EVERY MAN FOR HIMSELF

EVERY MAN
FOR
HIMSELF

Beryl Bainbridge

Carroll & Graf Publishers, Inc.
New York

For August, Esme and Inigo

First published in the UK in 1996 by Gerald Duckworth
& Co., Ltd.

First Carroll & Graf edition 1996

Carroll & Graf Publishers, Inc.
260 Fifth Avenue
New York, NY 10001

Library of Congress Cataloguing-In-Publication data for this
edition are available.

ISBN 0-7867-0349-0

Manufactured in the United States of America.

PROLOGUE

15th April 1912

He said, 'Save yourself if you can,' and I said firmly enough, though I was trembling and clutching at straws, 'I intend to. Will you stand at my side?' To which he replied, 'Remember, Morgan, not the height, only the drop, is terrible.' Then he walked away, gait unsteady, the cord of his robe trailing the deck.

I saw him once more, in those seconds which dragged by between my leap for the roof of the officers' house and the onrush of water that bore me aloft. He was standing against the rail, one arm hooked through to steady himself, and at first I didn't know him for he had taken off his spectacles; it was the velvet dressing gown I recognised.

He looked directly at me, all the time buffing his glasses on the hem of that plum-coloured robe, and I admit his occupation struck me as sensual. His hand, you see, was all but hidden beneath the material and I thought he was caressing himself. Death is such a lover's pinch that a man can be excused for prising himself free. Behind him on the horizon glimmered something I mistakenly took to be starlight.

I fancy he was smiling, but I can't be sure. Possibly I need to believe it ended that way, so that I can expel from my ears the ululation of grief which later pierced the glittering heavens.

The night was so still, the sea so calm, the moment so out of step with the catastrophe in progress that I made to join him, fluttered the fingers of my raised hand as though we were both guests at a social function and it was the most natural thing in the world to acknowledge the presence of a friend. My mouth even opened to shout some sort of greeting, though no words came.

I remember looking down at my right shoe, still inexplicably shiny with polish, as I prepared to take a stride towards that figure braced against the rail.

Then the water, first slithering, then tumbling, gushed us apart ...

ONE

At half-past four on the afternoon of 8th April 1912 – the weather was mild and hyacinths bloomed in window boxes – a stranger chose to die in my arms.

He was hung upon the railings of one of those grand houses in Manchester Square, arms spread like a scarecrow, the cloth of his city coat taking the strain. With his very first words he made it plain he wasn't overwhelmed by circumstances. 'I know who I am,' is what he clearly said. In the open window behind him a maid in a white cap stabbed flowers into a vase.

'It's as well to know oneself,' I replied, and walked on. I had reached the end of the street when I heard a shout; looking back I saw the unfortunate had shrugged himself out of his coat and was stumbling in my direction. His colourless face had eyebrows arched like a clown and lips that were turning blue.

'Please,' I said, as he pitched forward and clutched me round the waist. We both fell to our knees. Over the road a crocodile of Girl Guides sashayed sing-song through the ornamental gates of the public gardens.

I tried to free myself, but the man was drowning. His face was so close that his two eyes merged into one. I had thought he was drunk, yet his breath smelled sweet.

'Lay me down,' he whispered, and a tear rolled out of that one terrible eye and broke on the swell of his lip.

A nursemaid came down the sidewalk wheeling a per-ambulator. The infant was shrieking. I called out for assistance as the woman pushed past; there was a scrap of brown paper caught on the sole of her boot.

I laid him down as best I could, his head on the sidewalk. I would have taken off my jacket to serve as a cushion if he hadn't clung to my hands. His grip was fierce, as though someone unseen was dragging him in another direction. Then, arching a middle finger and foraging beneath the cuff of my shirt, he feather-dusted my beating pulse.

A sudden gust of wind shook the trees in the gardens and a prolonged sigh echoed along the street.

'The finger stroke of love,' he said, quite distinctly, and soon after, died.

Sometime during the minutes of his dying he had re-leased his hold on me, and, fumbling in his vest pocket, brought forth a small square of cardboard which he pressed against my heart.

After leaving the barber's shop, where the body had been carried by two constables, I found myself in possession of a snapshot of a Japanese woman peeping out from behind an embroidered fan. Retracing my steps I had every intention of giving it into the care of a constable, only to spy through the glass front of the shop the figure of the dead man seated in a barber's chair, a white cloth tied about his neck. I supposed he had been placed there, until a conveyance arrived, so as not to deter potential customers. His eyes were open and they were looking at me.

I went immediately to Princes Gate, packed my overnight bag and, leaving open the leaded window of my room to shift the tobacco smoke, closed the door quietly behind me. I paused in the corridor, did what I intended to do – it took but a moment – brushed the square of dust away with my sleeve and went to the head of the stairs.

As fate would have it, Cousin Jack was coming up as I descended. There followed a conversation of sorts, though my heart beat so loud I scarcely heard it. The evening sun shone through the stained glass window on the landing and set his beard ablaze.

'Ah,' he said, peering. 'It's you.'

'The very same,' I replied, dazzled.

'Are we well?' he asked.

'Pretty well.'

'Excellent,' he thundered, and stepped on past. One floor up the pet monkey hurled the length of its chain along the picture rail and leapt atop the banister.

Later I reproached myself for being so jumpy. Jack may have an eye for commerce but in most other respects he's monumentally blinkered. He is, after all, about his father's business. In all the weeks I'd stayed at that house in Princes Gate we had never once dined together, although it's true that we should have met for breakfast the morning after my arrival. On that occasion the cable working the dumb-waiter snapped between basement and dining room and the resulting cacophony of breaking china so unnerved me I fled before Jack appeared. At no time since had we occupied anything more spacious than the threshold of a room, he generally being on his way out as I entered, or the other way around. Beyond a grunt, possibly in reference to the weather, he had never acknowledged the cuckoo in his nest.

I wasn't entirely sure he even knew who I was. But then, he was nearly thirty years my senior and I no more than twelve years of age when he had last set eyes on me in the library of his father's brownstone on Madison Avenue.

I wouldn't like to give the impression that I thought badly of Jack. Quite the reverse; it was he who told my aunt it was time she stopped feeding me moonshine in regard to my beginnings. Up until then I knew little of my parents, beyond they were both headstrong and dead, my father two months before I was born and my mother, half-sister-in-law to my Uncle Morgan, three years after. I wasn't really bothered about the whys and wherefores, being well cared for by my aunt and my cousin Sissy, but often crazy images came into my head, either when I was on the point of dropping off to sleep or on the edge of waking, images of an old woman's face lying next to me on a soiled pillow. And then I'd come fully awake and scream the house down, begging for the window to be opened to let out the stench of her breath. Sometimes, when the dream had been really bad, Sissy would push up the balcony window and hold me there in my night-gown, telling me to suck in the night air, and those times I stopped breathing altogether, for when I looked down at the gas-lit street it had sunk beneath the sluggish waters of a canal.

I didn't find the truth all that upsetting, though Sissy wept for days. I was just thankful I hadn't slithered into the world on the wrong side of the tracks. As for the other grotesque happenings concerning my infant self, which I read about in brittle newspaper cuttings handed me by Jack soon after my twelfth birthday, why, they merely confirmed

14

a growing belief that I was special. I don't care to be misunderstood; I'm not talking about intellect or being singled out for great honours, simply that I was destined to be a participant rather than a spectator of singular events.

For instance, an hour before Amy Svenson hanged herself from the basement gate due to milk fever, I was marching my toy soldiers across the tiled lobby of the Madison Avenue house. Amy was scrubbing out the vestibule and when I started bawling – one of my tin Confederates had got caught in the castors of the hall table – she came in and sang me a lullaby. A bubble of soap burst in her hair as she took me on her knee. And when I was ten, staying down at the Van Hoppers' place, I met a man who blew his head off. I'd woken early one morning and roamed off on my own to the creek below the cemetery and there was Israel Wold, the half-baked tenant of the shack beyond the pines, on all fours, digging out the earth like he was a wild cat. He called out, 'Help me, pesky boy,' and obediently I crouched opposite and scrabbled at the ground. When the hole was deep enough he poured gunpowder into it from a sack slung from his belt and he said, 'Here I go and may the Lord go with me' and then he lay down with his head over the hole. I ran off because I knew he was cracked, and the next instant there was a noise like thunder and when I looked back I saw his old straw hat tossed into the misty sky as though someone had brought good news. Which is why I took the dead man in Manchester Square in my stride, though not quite.

That night I booked into a boarding house in Bloomsbury, and suffered accordingly. I suppose I could have gone down to Melchett's folk in Dorset, except the company they kept was real dull and their sofas awash with dogs.

Tuesday I'd gone with Laura Rothschild to a matinée of some play or other, let Melchett stand me dinner at the Carlton, staggered on with him to his club and then mislaid him at three o'clock in the morning outside the revolving doors of the Café Royal. In between I'd telegraphed my aunt, assuring her of my eagerness to see the family again, particularly Sissy who in my absence had produced a son and heir for her husband. It cost a few cents more but I also said I was in tip-top spirits. I wasn't, although I was truly bucked about Sissy and her boy. I recollect buying her a bunch of violets with the notion they might last the voyage home, only I shed them somewhere.

Melchett and I had planned to motor down to the ship together – his chauffeur had earlier taken charge of my luggage – but when I lost him at the Café Royal I was forced to catch the milk train from Waterloo, after which rattling journey through Woking, Winchester and Eastleigh I arrived at Southampton to spend a miserable hour perched on a coil of rope outside the Ocean Terminal, my only companion in the near darkness a boy endlessly sorting through the contents of a cardboard suitcase. I had plenty to think about; every time I hunched forward a corner of the picture frame inside my coat jabbed against my breastbone. Once, the boy called out to me, 'What's the time, mister?' but I didn't reply. He wore a white muffler about his throat and I thought of the dead man in the barber's chair.

Shortly after sunrise a straggling procession of men in

uniform approached Gate 4 and crossed the railway tracks on to Ocean Road. It was then the doors of the South Western Hotel opened and I was able to order a breakfast of overdone kippers. At that hour there were only three other guests in the dining room, two of whom had their backs to me. Of these, one was a woman soberly dressed and the other a stoutly built fellow sitting alone in an alcove, one hand constantly hovering about the string of an oblong box lying beside his chair. The third occupant, middle-aged and wearing spectacles, sat opposite the woman. His face, otherwise fleshy and undistinguished, was remarkable for a mouth whose lower lip was scored through as though by a slash from a knife; split thus, it gave him a roguish appearance. Leaning backwards in his chair, he talked in so distinctive a voice and with such authority that several times I caught the drift of what he said. I took him to be a lawyer, for he seemed to be conducting an interrogation rather than a conversation.

'Are you sure that you have the will?... What makes you think you possess the strength?... What will you do with success when it comes?' To which last question the woman replied barely above a whisper. I have the knack of concentration and although a waiter was poking the coals into flame and plates were clattering in the kitchens beyond the green baize door, I heard her plain. 'Why, I shall be happy,' is what she said.

It was then her companion looked across and met my eye. He was smiling in such a jovial fashion, that, taken off guard, I pretended to be engrossed in the view from the window. By now the crimson dawn had torn to rags and the

17

dull sky was all but blotted out by the giant funnels towering above the roofs of the shipping offices below. I guess there must have been a breeze for I remember watching the flutter of the signal flags.

It struck me, even then, that the stranger with the scarred lip was someone I might usefully cultivate. There was a robustness about him, an arrogance that had nothing to do with money, and if I hadn't felt so liverish I'd have responded to that first zestful overture. I'm not, or rather I wasn't, the sort of fellow who sees the point in keeping his distance, particularly if it's likely to lead to amusement.

The man with the oblong package was the first to leave. He too looked at me and nodded as he passed by. His cool acknowledgement and the graceful manner in which he manoeuvred his way between the tables surprised me; one always expects fat men of a certain class to be both clumsy and lacking in confidence. In spite of myself, I nodded in return. At that instant the clock on the mantelpiece struck the hour and the woman rose from her chair. The stout man reached the door and half turned. The expression on his face was so open, his feelings of admiration, if not downright desire, so apparent, that I too looked at the woman. She was singularly tall for her sex, statuesque in build, and wore a tailored coat made of some dark material with a touch of cheap fur at throat and wrists. From her low-brimmed hat escaped a wave of bright hair. I have no early recollection of the beauty of her features, the Roman nose, the width between her pale eyes, only of the translucency of her skin. It would be true to say, if couched a shade poetically, that she had a complexion so luminous in its perfection that it was like gazing upon a pearl.

For perhaps five seconds the three of us remained fixated, he looking at her, she looking at him, myself regarding first one then the other. He was hatless and a bead of sweat rolled from beneath the black curls lolling on his brow. Then the fourth spectator, leaning even further backward in his seat, called out, 'My word, life is a tragedy, what?' It was such a knowing, insolent intrusion that I coloured up.

Minutes later he too quit the room. This time I made out I was studying the breakfast menu. As he passed he gave a little bark of a cough, doubtless to draw my attention. I didn't look up; in my present state of lethargy I feared I might disappoint him. Though not vain, I'm aware my outward appearance raises expectations.

When he'd gone I remained for an hour or more in the empty dining room, during which time the third class train from Waterloo puffed up the tracks of West Road and disgorged its steerage passengers alongside White Star Dock. I took little interest in the massive liner that was soon to carry me home, though in her beauty she was as deserving of attention as the tall woman who had recently left the hotel. More so, for in a small way, albeit very small, I'd helped in her creation. That being said, my thoughts were mostly of my mother who had never been closer to my heart.

Dreaming there, my mind racing the clouds above Southampton Water, I resolved, not for the first time, to spend the next few days pursuing fitness of mind and body; a visit to the swimming pool and squash court each morn-

19

ing, the library in the afternoon followed by two courses at dinner, absolutely no alcohol and retirement by ten o'clock at the latest. No sooner had I dwelt on the satisfaction to be gained from such a puritanical regime than I was compelled to order a brandy. I wasn't irresolute by nature, merely shaken at the prospect.

I saw the man with the split lip again when I was searching for Melchett's automobile. He was talking to J.S. Seefax, a second cousin of my aunt's and a crashing bore, always rambling on about his early manhood in Georgia when as an agent for the Confederate Government he'd helped run the blockade of Europe. I fancy he saw me too, for they both turned in my direction, but at that moment, the first class passenger train having just drawn in, I glimpsed Van Hopper on the platform. He was with two other fellows, one of whom I knew slightly and didn't much care for. The previous month, at a party given by Laura Rothschild, knowing I was related to J. Pierpont Morgan – for whom I'm named – he'd traded on a dubious connection within minutes of our being introduced. 'My grandmother,' he had boasted, 'was a great friend of Mr Morgan's. In her girlhood, of course.' He had the audacity to wink. I'm not above snobbishness – my own beginnings were lamentable enough – but I detest crawlers, or rather I despise a too evident regard for birth and position.

Later we'd crossed swords at a picnic beside the Thames on the occasion of the Oxford and Cambridge boat race. When the first boat sank he let out a roar of delight, and upon the second taking on water he ran up and down the bank, crowing and flinging his boater into the air. I told him to keep quiet but he wouldn't, at which I challenged him to put his fists up, only to have him flopping down in the grass and waving his legs about like a beetle. I guess he was drunk.

Van Hopper said I looked pretty well done in, though he himself was unshaven and his boots in need of a blacking brush. He demanded to know what had happened to me the night before; apparently he and Melchett had spent a good three hours waiting for me to show up at the Café Royal.

I was fond of Hopper, though distrustful. However close, one should always be wary of those with a different perspective on the past. My sense of injustice is ... was ... sharper than his and I believe in retribution. Nor do I mistake the limits of my own horizons for those of the world. Van Hopper's round eyes and pink cheeks give him away; he has ... had ... the face of a child.

'I was there,' I told him.

'The head waiter thought he saw you, or someone very like. You were clutching a bunch of dead pansies and warbling the chorus from *The Barber of Seville*.' He turned to his beetle friend smirking at his shoulder. 'I believe you've met Archie Ginsberg.'

'It can't have been me,' I protested. 'I was in no mood for singing.'

Hopper's people and mine were connected by marriage, and equally disconnected in that all our lives our respective father figures had preferred to spend time with women other than their wives. It was worse for Hopper, of course, seeing I had no mother who could be betrayed. It's only recently that my uncle has discovered a sense of family

21

unity – old age is remarkable for its lurch towards sentimentality – and in childhood Hopper and I had spent most part of every summer at the house of his maternal grandmother in Maine. When I see Hopper in my head, it is with knees drawn up to his chest, swinging out on the weeping branches of the dusty willow that grew in the shallows of the lake at Warm Springs.

Grown, we'd roomed together at Harvard and I had hoped he and Sissy might make a go of it, although he was too much the loafer and she a sight too serious-minded for it to come to anything. She's only a girl, yet her intelligence is formidable. They'd spent a lot of time battling it out on the tennis court, often in moonlight, but she was never enamoured enough to let him win. In my view her husband Whitney is more of a slouch than Hopper. Against that, I have to take Sissy's word for it he has the sort of eyelashes to set a girl's heart pounding.

If Van Hopper had been unaccompanied I would willingly have stayed at his side; as it was, I took advantage of the crush on the platform to slip away and board on my own. Several times I was greeted by people I knew, lastly by the Carters of Philadelphia who stood at the foot of the first class gangway supporting a swaying J.S. Seefax at either elbow.

'Morgan,' Mrs Carter called out when she saw me, waving her free hand imploringly.

'What fun,' I cried back, and clambered upwards, damned if I was going to be saddled with helping the old dodderer to his stateroom.

As it happened, I wouldn't have been able to, not without

map and compass. I had worked as an apprentice draughts-man in the design offices of Harland and Wolff for eleven months prior to the launch of the ship, but only on a section of E deck aft, and she had eight decks, each in excess of eight hundred feet in length. Unfamiliar as I was with the general layout of the huge vessel, it was with considerable difficulty and after many wrong turnings that I found my berth. Entering amidships on B deck and foolishly avoiding the Grand Staircase, I was confronted with such bewildering stretches of passageways and companionways, each thronged with a confusion of people, that I got into the wrong elevator and was first transported, packed like a sardine, down to the racquets courts on G deck, and then swept too far up and spilled out, starboard side, into the gymnasium on the boat deck. Here, a singular sight awaited, that of the stout man who had earlier breakfasted in the South Western Hotel, still clutching that oblong box and with hat now jammed over his eyes, seated astride a mechanical camel. I learned later he'd been persuaded into this undignified pose by a photographer from the *Illustrated London News*.

When I eventually reached my accommodation on C deck it was a relief to find my luggage not only installed but in the process of being unpacked by a steward who had sensibly made enquiries as to my status. The resulting infor-mation rendered him suitably deferential, yet not sufficiently so as to arouse contempt; I like people to know their place, just as long as I'm not required to step on them. He said his name was McKinlay and in common with his kind he was more than eager to discuss my fellow passengers. As a proud native of some Scottish village with an unpronounceable name, rather than a product of the huddled masses of my adopted country, his approach was almost subtle. On my complaining that I'd had the devil of a job getting to my cabin, he expressed astonishment and promised to mention it to the chief steward.

'Very mysterious, sir,' he said, 'seeing we're at full muster and fewer passengers than expected owing to cancellations. Mr Vanderbuilt, sir, telegraphed only yesterday, although his luggage and valet are already aboard. I gather his mother, Mrs Dressler, has an aversion to maiden voyages. Same with Mr Frick, sir, and family, down as joining us at Cherbourg … now there's a gentleman and no mistake.'

'Yes, indeed,' I agreed; my endorsement was insincere. When I graduated from Harvard my uncle had approached Frick with a view to my being slotted into the steel magnate's empire. Choosing to sound me out in the vulgar château he had built for himself on Fifth Avenue rather than his office, he put me at a disadvantage, for his drawing room was so gloomy with panelled oak and the windows so obscured with velvet drapes that I failed to notice his sleeping Pomeranian. Paws stepped upon, it scuttled squealing under the ottoman. The mishap undid me, for though I expressed concern, indeed sorrow, it was reported that my mouth smiled. There followed a brief lecture in which 'bad blood' was mentioned in connection with certain incidents concerning my early life. My aunt, when told of his diatribe, wept. My uncle, after testily bidding me to be more careful where I trod, advised me to accept Frick's recommendation that I seek employment in the gold mines of South Africa. Mercifully my aunt intervened.

'Mr Vanderbilt's suite,' continued the steward, 'has been taken over by a gentleman who was to have travelled second class. It's rumoured he comes from Manchester.'

'That's in the north,' I said, as though I wasn't sure.

'Indeed it is, sir, and a very prosperous city. The gentleman in question is in the clothing business.' Here the steward tried to relieve me of my overcoat. I shook him off; the picture frame was still tucked against my ribs.

'May I say, sir,' he blabbered on, 'how sorry we are not to have the pleasure of your uncle's company this trip. Business commitments, I shouldn't wonder.'

'Mr Morgan,' I said, 'is a glutton for work,' and feared I sounded too dry. My uncle, possibly at that moment, was strolling the beach at Aix-les-Bains in the company of his mistress. 'Mr Frick,' I added, 'is equally burdened.'

'As I understand it, sir,' the steward replied, 'his is in the nature of a domestic dilemma. His lady wife has broken her ankle.'

Presently he left me. I took the painting from my coat and propped it on the dressing table. The girl's eyes were less searching than when gazing from the wall of the corridor at Princes Gate. Nor did she seem as pretty, her nose a shade too tilted, her jaw-line a little too heavy. I looked for a likeness in my own face in the glass, and found none.

The steward returned with bath-towels. He said two young ladies had arrived to take up the adjoining stateroom. 'Daughter of a baronet.' he confided, 'travelling with a companion. Both on the excitable side.'

25

I laid the painting on the bed and went in search of Melchett.

*

It was some minutes to noon when I made my way up the ship by means of the Grand Staircase. Judging by the number of people hurrying downwards, departure was imminent. I was nearly knocked off my feet by Mr Ismay who fairly ran past trailing three pale children. Behind, wearing the melancholy expression habitual to men assured of the fulfilment of cherished hopes, loped Thomas Andrews, managing director and chief designer of the White Star Line.

Although Andrews didn't stop, he hailed me by name, followed by the flung observation that it was good to see me and we should talk later. Immensely hard working and reserved to a fault, he had more than once paused beside my desk on one of his fleeting visits to the draughtsmen's shed at Queen's Island. The work I'd been put to was hardly worthy of comment, let alone praise – my uncle had a regrettable belief in the harmful effects of nepotism and I was engaged in specifications concerning wash-basins in the third class accommodation areas – but Andrews had never failed to convey appreciation. It was only to be expected, of course, that he should take a special interest in my progress, seeing I was nephew to the owner of the shipping line, yet I fancied he liked me for my own sake.

Gratified at the encounter I came out on A deck and by dint of persistence managed to secure a position at the rail some yards below the bridge. I was wedged between two ladies, one wielding a parasol, the other laughing.

There was now but one gangway remaining, at the foot of which the master-at-arms was preventing a dozen or more working men from boarding. I guess they had dallied too long in the nearest public house and arrived too late to sign on. One of them flung his kit upwards, and, attempting to duck under the officer's arm, was sent staggering from a shove to the chest.

'Shame,' murmured the woman with the parasol, and then she too began to laugh.

From where I stood I could see Captain Smith talking with the quartermaster on the deck above. I liked Smith, though I wasn't sure I got his measure. I was sixteen when I first met him, the time my aunt had taken me to Europe on the SS *Adriatic*, then under his command. He'd owned a drooling dog which I took to exercising each day, throwing it ginger biscuits on the promenade deck. Being young and in need of sensation I often hoped the biscuit would skitter overboard and the dog leap to follow, though had it done so I expect I would have howled with the best of them. Smith came up one morning and caught me at play. He said nothing but I know he rumbled me because that night at dinner he hooked the dog's lead over my chair. On the same voyage six of the crew were caught looting the first class baggage hold. My aunt reported a lost vanity case which had belonged to her mother, Everyone said how ugly such behaviour was and how an abuse of trust harmed the per-petrator almost as much as the victim. My aunt held that the rich, having a heightened sense of property, were bound to feel such betrayals more keenly than the poor. Later she discovered she'd left the case at home.

As I watched, the quartermaster put up his hand to grasp the lanyard. A unified wail of anticipation rose from the quayside, to be drowned in the ship's awesome boom of farewell as steam gushed from the giant whistles half-way up the forward funnels. They blasted twice more, scattering the seabirds wheeling through the black smoke billowing from the tugs now straining to drag the *Titanic* from dock to river. A weak sun came out and the paintwork glittered.

The hysterical woman on my left expressed disappointment at the lack of ceremony, there being neither bands to serenade our leaving nor the customary salutes from vessels berthed nearby. 'I expected more of a show,' she complained.

For myself, I was past caring one way or the other, being in that disembodied state of mind induced by a sleepless night and a double brandy. As the ship slid away and the town, nudged by its purple forest, slipped along the horizon, I drifted somewhere above the giddy circling of the smoke-wreathed gulls.

I remember the woman with the parasol asking if it wasn't grand to see the look of gratitude on the castaway's face – she identified him as a stoker – now that his kit-bag had been flung down to him on the dock, and I said yes, yes, pretty darn grand, although I was no longer looking at the quay but one deck below to where the man with the split lip stood beside the woman who had been his companion in the hotel. She was clearly agitated, leaning at a dangerous angle over the rail and gesticulating wildly. A breeze blew up, threatening the stability of her hat, and he took her by the elbows and forced her round to face him. He actually shook her, at which she crumpled. Awkwardly, for she was at least six inches the taller, she hid her face in his shoulder. He spoke to her then and in spite of the hullabaloo all around I had the curious notion I heard what he said. *'All is not lost. There is always another way.'*

I came to myself then, and some moments later Charlie Melchett clapped me on the back, full of apologies for the mishap of the night before.

'I did look for you,' he shouted. 'I sent the car round to Princes Gate at four o'clock this morning.'

'My fault,' I bellowed. 'Don't give it a thought.'

'They said they hadn't seen you for two days. Where the devil have you been staying?'

'I told you the whole story last night,' I said.

'You went through the revolving doors like a dervish, but when Hopper–' He broke off and tugged at my arm. 'Look, there's my mother. She's seen us.'

I waved dutifully at the onlookers side-stepping to keep pace with us, though it was impossible to distinguish one face among so many. I was genuinely fond of kind Lady Melchett – but then, almost all mothers I have known have been kind to me. Besides, we had now reached that point where the dock waters met the upper reaches of the sea and the ship was beginning a ninety-degree turn to port. A tremor was felt on deck as the propellers churned to combat the incoming tide.

The nearby docks were full of ships, including the *Olympic*, laid up on account of the recently ended miners' strike.

It was the strike and the uncertainty of a sailing date that had caused the cancellations. My aunt had cabled that I should make it to France and transfer to the *Mauretania*, but as my baggage had already gone on ahead and I hadn't wanted to miss the fun of travelling with Melchett and Van Hopper I'd stuck to my plans. More to the point, I knew Thomas Andrews would be aboard.

The *Olympic* was berthed in the Test Docks alongside the SS *New York*, whose stern we were now approaching. A man in a bowler hat ran back and forth across her poop deck waving his arms windmill fashion. As we drew level both ships rocked under our swell; I clearly saw the tethering ropes slacken, then grow taut.

'Promise to shoot me,' shouted Melchett, 'if you ever catch me sporting a bowler at sea.'

Some people heard what they thought were revolver shots when the *New York* broke her moorings. The man on the poop leapt in shock as her hawsers whipped the air. Hissing, the crowd surged backwards. Hopper later swore he'd seen a woman lashed round the waist and spun like a top across the quay, but I doubt it; she would surely have been cut in two. Drawn by the *Titanic*'s displacement of water, the *New York* began to swing towards our bows.

I don't think the womenfolk on either side of me were conscious of the danger, indeed, judging from their redoubled squeals and the abandoned manner in which the parasol swirled about my head, the incident appeared merely to provide that missing element of showmanship.

The tugs having got lines on her, the *New York* was nosed

out of our way. All the same, it took an hour or more, at the end of which the *Titanic*'s bugler, sounding a delayed serving of the midday meal, rose from deck to deck blowing 'The Roast Beef of Old England'. Melchett and I, neither of us being hungry, went on a tour of the ship.

An hour later we had got no further than the smoke-room. As Melchett drolly remarked, we had plenty of time and the ship was unlikely to go anywhere without us. That geek Ginsberg was there; fortunately he was engaged in conversation with one of the Taft cousins and kept his distance. Quite suddenly I felt immensely cheerful, and it had nothing to do with the lager beer we were drinking. The feeling took me by surprise as up until then I hadn't known I was miserable. One moment it had been the hardest thing in the world to attempt the faintest of smiles, and the next there was this almighty rush of well-being that had me grinning inanely. I expect it had much to do with being in Melchett's company. I didn't know him as intimately as I knew Hopper, which meant there was none of that careless-ness bordering on contempt usual between friends of long standing. All at once, it struck me he was the sort of fellow one could confide in.

He was enthusing over the magnificence of the ship, comparing it in concept and visionary grandeur to the great cathedrals of Chartres and Notre Dame. 'A cathedral,' he reiterated, waving his cheroot in the direction of the stained glass above the bar, 'constructed of steel and capable of carrying a congregation of three thousand souls across the Atlantic.'

'I took a picture from my uncle's house,' I said. 'That's why you couldn't find me this morning.'

'Just think of it,' he crowed. 'All this mass and speed and yet she moves so gracefully she doesn't even tilt the drink in one's glass.' He thumped the arm of his chair at the wonder of it.

'I moved into a hotel because I stole a picture, Charlie,' I said, and immediately regretted the correction.

For a moment I thought he hadn't heard me. He sat there, one side of his blond head darkened by the ruby glow of the mahogany wall, eyes bright with pleasure. 'What picture?' he asked.

'Of my mother. Painted before I was born.'

'It wasn't a painting,' he said. 'Just a photograph. You insisted on passing it round after we caught up with Van Hopper at my club. You spun a yarn about it having been given you by some poor chap who ended up dead in a barber's chair. We couldn't get any sense out of you.'

'There *was* a dead man –'

'And it couldn't have been your mother ... not unless she was Japanese.'

At that, I felt more cheerful than ever, for while I'd eased my conscience I'd miraculously avoided censure. All the same, there was a corner of me that wished he had listened.

Shortly after, Melchett ordered champagne to toast the start of our voyage. 'To being alive,' he said, thrusting his glass towards the ceiling. 'To being young, to being lucky enough to be here at such a time.' Following this outburst of sentiment, he grew pink; he was, after all, British.

I own I felt protective of him; he was such a boy. I'd never had a brother, any more than I'd known a mother or a father. Women can nurture anything small enough, including animals, but I reckon men need someone of their own sex to arouse an instinct free of possessiveness. Charlie was nineteen years old and I twenty-two, and those three years might have been thirty if a gap in innocence could be measured.

We drank just enough to heighten our perceptions, so that when we began our inspection of the ship I fancy we'd loosened that grey veil of sophistication common to our kind.

Melchett was keen on visiting E deck, mostly on account of a broad alleyway, known to the crew by the name of Scotland Road after some street in Liverpool, which ran the length of the vessel. He had visited the northern city as a child, he eagerly told me, on the occasion of a horse running in his grandfather's colours in the Grand National steeple-chase. I did tell him, knowledgeable as I was in regards to plumbing in the steerage accommodation, that it was unlikely he would find the thoroughfare thronged with race-horses, but he was adamant. We duly descended by elevator and roamed up and down a tiled corridor intersected by iron staircases leading to working departments of indescribable dullness. Melchett, trying hard to remain animated, wilted. 'What is the point,' he complained, 'of giving names to places that bear no resemblance to the past?'

'The point is,' I stressed, 'that they draw attention to the origin of the reference. Think of Waterloo station.'

After which exchange we fortunately encountered a young seaman who was persuaded to conduct us over the lower decks. Reluctant at first, then swayed by the promise of a generous tip, he led us below. Though stunted in growth, his eyes shone with intelligence. He said his name was Riley and his home town Liverpool, where he lived with his 'Mam' and five siblings. Considerably bucked at the coincidence, Melchett boasted he knew the town quite well. 'My grandfather,' he said, 'owned a horse that finished second in the Grand National of 1901 ... I can't for the life of me remember its name.'

'Me Dad,' replied Riley, 'had a donkey called Dickey-Sam that pulled a rag and bone cart.' Melchett said that was interesting, and turned pink again.

Apart from a certain casualness of manner Riley proved to be the best of guides, for though the English he spoke could have benefited from an interpreter his knowledge of the ship was profound and his appreciation infectious. On F deck, starboard side, beneath which the main engines were housed, he delivered a lecture on their capacity and capabilities. The vessel, I understood him to inform us, was powered by two four-cylinder, triple expansion, reciprocating steam engines. Each could deliver 15,000 horsepower at 75 revolutions, producing a speed of 21 knots. Aft of these, a low-pressure turbine recycled steam from the main engines to drive the three propellers. He was wrong in this last assumption, in that it was only the central propeller that was thus driven, but I held my tongue.

'There's also four 400 kilowatt steam-powered generators,' he said, 'with dynamos capable of providing enough electricity to work the machinery controlling the winches, cranes, passenger and service lifts, heaters, cookers, watertight doors, the internal telephone exchange and the Marconi wireless set to a range of 350 miles. It can go further at night,' he concluded. 'Though I'm buggered if I know why.'

Melchett, shamelessly taking advantage of his enthusiasm, pressed to be allowed a glimpse of such wonders. A glimpse was all we got; barely a minute after we reached G deck and Riley had dragged back the iron door of Number 1 engine room we were approached by an assistant engineer and ordered about our business. Brief as the moment had been we had nonetheless clearly seen the awesome monster rearing on splayed legs from the glittering avenue below, its gigantic head vibrating inside its steel helmet, its thunderous intestines of lubricated pistons and crank-shafts pounding and pumping in perpetual motion.

Riley was sent packing. I'm ashamed to say neither Melchett nor I put in a word for him, nor was there time to palm him his tip. Escorted by the engineer we were returned by twists and turns and much tapping up of metal stairs to E deck, where, after sternly reminding us that unauthorised explorations of engine and boiler rooms were against company safety rules, he left us. I could have told him who I was and put him in his place but was loath to puncture his sense of self-importance, having had my own pricked on numerous occasions, and with more cause, by my Uncle Morgan.

Melchett and I remained silent while we continued our inspection of the ship, and when it was done and we had sunk into the leather armchairs in the foyer of A deck we still had no words. It wasn't the lavish furnishings of the public rooms, the doors inlaid with mother of pearl, the panelled corridors of oak and maple, the shimmer of gilt and brass and cut glass that made us catch our breath, anymore than the twenty-one-light candelabra hung from the massive dome above the sweep of that imperial staircase. We had spent our lives in splendid houses and grand hotels and for us there was nothing new under the sun, nothing that is, in the way of opulence; it was the sublime thermodynamics of the *Titanic*'s marine engineering that took us by the throat. Dazzled, I was thinking that if the fate of man was connected to the order of the universe, and if one could equate the scientific workings of the engines with just such a reciprocal universe, why then, nothing could go wrong with my world.

I don't know what Melchett was thinking, beyond he was pale and his left knee was bouncing up and down as though in imitation of those connecting rods oscillating below the water line.

Just then, old man Seefax called out my name. He was tottering through the doors of the promenade deck supported between a bell-hop boy and the man with the split lip. Behind strutted the stout individual last seen on the mechanical camel. I jumped up and offered my chair to Seefax.

'Morgan,' he said, 'why the devil isn't your uncle aboard?'

'Business,' I said.

'Nonsense. He was cruising the Nile a week ago.'

'Which precipitated an attack of the gout,' I said. 'It came on suddenly.'

I was about to perjure myself further when my attention was distracted by the sight of the statuesque woman ascending the main staircase. She was waving her hand in my direction.

'Have you met Scurra?' asked Seefax. 'Your uncle knows him.'

'He does not *know* me,' corrected the man with the split lip. 'But we were acquainted in the past.'

'Pleased to meet you, Mr Scurra,' I said, holding out my hand.

'Not *Mr*,' he replied. 'In my experience such prefixes erect barriers. Haven't you found that to be the case?'

He was watching me closely through those heavy spectacles; his eyes were nearer black than brown.

I said, 'I believe someone is looking for you.'

He glanced over his shoulder and saw the woman. She called out, 'We're nearly at Cherbourg ... he will surely be there.'

'I hope so,' he said, 'for your sake,' and turned back to me.

She waited there a moment before going out on deck, as if expecting him to join her. I must admit I was puzzled; for all his ease of manner and air of authority, no gentleman would treat his wife in such a churlish manner, let alone a mistress.

As though he read my thoughts, he exclaimed, 'Yet another damsel in distress. They're everywhere, dear boy,' and laughed so boisterously I couldn't help smiling.

Perching himself on the arm of Melchett's chair he took off his spectacles and began to rub at them with his hand-kerchief. Looking up at me, he said, 'I understand you have been working as a designer under Thomas Andrews.'

'Simply as a draughtsman,' I replied, somewhat stiffly.

37

'Concerned mainly with the specifications of bathtubs.' Even then I wanted to impress him but had a sixth sense he would see through the attempt. Without his spectacles I saw his eyes were grey, not brown.

He said, 'Andrews is a curious man. Unlike many who regard succession as a right, he believes in proving himself. I find that very boring, don't you? He also believes in fate.'

'Fate,' I echoed.

'The sentence of the Gods. A comforting idea, don't you think, in that it leaves the individual blameless?'

'Yes, indeed,' I said, though I hardly knew what I was agreeing with. It wasn't comfortable, talking to him. Quite apart from keeping one's gaze from off his damaged lip, everything he said was expressed in such a way as to require an answer, and a considered one at that. He had no small talk.

'Melchett and I have been down to the engine rooms,' I blurted. 'We were both bowled over.' I nudged Melchett's shoulder, but though he glanced up he was too polite to disturb Seefax's rambling conversation. Scurra was watching the fat man who had adopted the dandified stance of a ballet dancer, heel of one foot thrust at an angle against the other, head turned theatrically aside in the direction of the doors through which the tall woman had gone. 'I wouldn't care,' I said, 'to get in the way of such machinery. It could slice one in half.'

'My mouth,' Scurra said, 'is the result of a discourse with a macaw while walking through a department store in Cape Town –'

'Forgive me,' I stammered. 'I didn't mean –'

'I was but six years old at the time. My mother was intent on buying material for a dress. She had let go my hand and walked on ahead. The bird had eyes like marbles. I reached upwards to stroke it – it was so close I smelt the sawdust on its unused wings. *All is not lost*, it croaked, and I cockily replied, *What has gone missing*? One should always attempt to understand what is being asked of one, don't you think? … at which, hopping along its perch it swooped down and pecked my mouth. I have been told my blood spouted out like liquid from a teapot.'

He replaced his spectacles, stood up with a mock sigh and taking the fat man by the elbow announced it was time for a turn on deck. The fat man seemed to be in some sort of trance; he said not a word as he was led to the elevator.

I tried to find out from J.S. Seefax what Scurra did for a living and in what way he might be acquainted with my uncle. The old man was vague. 'I think we met in Boston …' he said, 'or perhaps it was Paris. One goes to so many places.'

'And who is the man he was with?'

'What man?' he asked, and that was as far as I got.

I returned to my stateroom, rang for the steward and instructed him to call me at five thirty. He enquired whether I would require lemonade to revive me on waking, or something stronger. Stung, I ordered tea.

My room was done out in the style of Louis XVI; there was a feeble engraving of the Bastille hung on the picture rail above the writing desk. On an impulse I removed it from its hook and replaced it with the painting of my mother.

I stretched out on the bed and hoped she would watch over me, but her eyes looked at some point beyond my head. Absent to the last, I thought, and slipped into sleep.

*

Dinner that evening was a boisterous affair. Ours was a small world and between the soup and the fish we were all constantly bobbing up and down to acknowledge people we knew; but for the intermittent and minute flickerings of the electric lights we might have been dining at the Ritz in Paris. The Theyers stopped at our table, the Daniels, Mrs Snyder, the Speddens of Tuxedo Park, Colonel Gracie, jolly Mrs Hogeboom with the excessively rich and eccentric Mrs James Brown, her bridge crony from Denver, in tow. As usual, the latter was dressed inappropriately and wore a gigantic hat across whose brim languished an entire stuffed bird. Colonel Astor and his young bride passed by without a nod, leaving Ginsberg on his feet with hand held foolishly out. He said he knew Vincent, the Colonel's eldest son, and had often fenced with him.

'Verbally or with foils?' asked wicked Molly Dodge, but he ignored her.

The new Mrs Astor was pale and tall like her husband, and both looked as if they'd barely finished a thundering row. They'd been travelling Europe for months, waiting for the scandal of his divorce to die down. They joined Captain Smith's party, alongside the Strauses and Bruce Ismay, and sat as though exhausted, he nearing fifty, his long gloomy nose nudging his moustaches, she barely nineteen, her flower head drooping on the stalk of her neck.

Benjamin Guggenheim had come aboard at Cherbourg with his mistress, Kitty Webb. I'd danced with Kitty once at some charity ball and found her touching; she'd confessed to biting her nails. She had pouting blue eyes, a small mouth and a mother, so it was said, who had hoed corn. Guggenheim had picked her out of the chorus line of *Naughty Marietta*. It was spread about that he'd fallen for her when she'd burst into tears and run off stage in the middle of the song 'Ah Sweet Mystery of Life'. As Guggenheim wasn't famed for his sensitivity this was taken to be a tall yarn.

When Kitty paused at our table she brushed my cheek with her hand.

'Morgan,' she breathed. 'How thrilling to see you.'

Ginsberg boasted he knew her, of course. He held she truly loved Guggenheim and that it wasn't doing her a power of good. I thought that was phooey judging by the size of the sapphires in the necklace about her throat, and said so. Wallis Ellery gave me one of her glances and pronounced it a vulgar observation, which shrivelled me, though I laughed it off.

A curious interchange took place when Melchett leapt up at the approach of a woman escorted by a pink porpoise of a man. He was about to greet them when the woman cried out, 'Our name is Morgan.'

'Yes, indeed,' said her companion, adding with exaggerated emphasis, 'We are always known as Mr and Mrs Morgan.'

Melchett looked fairly taken aback, at which the woman

41

pressed her finger against his lips and said, 'Charlie dear, not a word,' and swept on.

'How very rum,' said Melchett.

'What Morgans are those?' I asked mystified.

'Not Morgan at all,' he replied. 'That was Lord and Lady Duff Gordon.'

There were eight of us at table; Hopper, Melchett, Ginsberg, George Dodge, his half-sister Molly, the Ellery sisters and myself. Ida Ellery wasn't pretty, which is possibly why she was so good-natured and easy to be with. We were all madly in love with her sister Wallis, who was as clever as Sissy and absolutely unobtainable. In Wallis's company it was impossible not to stare, and dangerous, for if she caught you and was in the mood to look back her gaze was so level and her expression so mocking it could turn one to stone. She had warm dark eyes and a pale full mouth, and just above her lip there was the faintest fuzz of down which glinted chestnut where the light touched. No one ever dared flirt with Wallis. Dancing with her was like holding cut glass; Hopper got it about right when he complained she made him feel he left finger marks.

We much admired the dining saloon, all, that is, except Wallis. In her opinion it was a travesty to do up a room in the Jacobean style and then paint the woodwork white. As for the cream vases stacked with lilies, why, it made her feel she was at a funeral.

'It does smell like a florist's,' agreed daffy Ida, who would have sold her soul to keep the peace.

'It's not the lilies,' exclaimed Molly Dodge, 'it's Ginsberg.

42

He's been to the barber's shop,' and she cruelly wrinkled her prominent nose.

'It's the latest French cologne,' he told her, not in the least put out.

'You won't catch Morgan setting foot in the barber's,' said Hopper, and launched into a highly embellished version of my encounter with the dying man in Manchester Square.

'He didn't die in the chair,' I said. 'Nor was he covered in blood. He died rather peacefully, probably from heart failure.'

'How did you know he was dead?' asked Wallis.

'Because he died in my arms ... in the street.'

She shivered, but persisted. 'But how did you know? What did he look like ...?'

'He was quite tall,' I said. 'And he had dark hair.'

'Not *him*,' she said. 'Death. What did death look like?'

I noticed her hands. She was brushing one tapering finger against the pulse in her wrist. *One should always attempt to understand what is being asked of one*, I thought.

'As though a light had gone out,' I said, and would have told her more if her sister Ida hadn't shuddered and begged me to talk about something less sinister.

We all drank a great deal. When I first heard my voice getting louder I was angry at myself, but by then it was too late. Most of us had got used to alcohol fairly early on in life. At Harvard only the swots and the athletes kept themselves pure; members of the smart set were expected to drink themselves under the table.

Ginsberg grew heated pretty quick. He and George

43

Dodge had begun a discussion on Germany and in no time at all the conversation had somehow switched from the superiority of the German navy to Ginsberg ranting on about there being only two overwhelming impulses, hunger and the sexual instinct. Out of respect for the girls, and timidity, George stopped disagreeing as soon as he saw which way the wind was blowing, but Ginsberg wouldn't be quieted. 'Hunger,' he shouted, chopping at the cheese on his plate, 'is easily satisfied, but the other ...' and here he breathed through his nose like a horse.

'There is another impulse,' I said. 'Boredom. Which is never absent when you're around.'

'That isn't an impulse,' he retorted. 'Merely a feeling.'

I didn't like playing the boss-man, but with George, who was always so eager to merge into the crowd, it was unavoidable. And it did shut Ginsberg up.

Not that the girls turned a hair; judging by the serene manner in which she surveyed the room Wallis hadn't even been listening. As for Molly Dodge, I doubt she could ever be put out of countenance. Right from a child she'd been sassy, unlike George, who was always a scaredy-cat and remained so. He'd been a weekly boarder at St Mark's, which wasn't usual – a delicate constitution was the excuse but we reckoned his father wanted to keep a bully rein on him – and on Friday nights he travelled the half-hour home on the family's private train. The Dodges lived in Manchester-by-the-Sea, at Apple Trees, a colonial mansion on the North Shore, and sometimes George invited me along for the weekend. He and I weren't great friends; it was just good to get away from school once in a while, and besides,

George was needy and I felt I owed it to him seeing I was fortunate enough never to have been crushed by circumstances. In the fall it was misty along the shore and all through dinner one heard the melancholy wail of fog-horns and every damn time Molly would whisper, 'Was that a fart, Morgan?'

Ginsberg kept refilling my glass. I'll say this for him, blatherskite or not, he wasn't a sulker, and after all, he'd only voiced what the rest of us felt. Most of our time was spent thinking what we might do with women if only we had the chance. There were houses we could go to, of course, but with girls of our own set there was never the slightest opportunity of trying out even a little of what we'd learnt, which rendered us incapable of behaving naturally in their company. In our best moments, mercifully dominant, we thought of them as sisters or mothers and treated them accordingly; in our worst they were always whores, white and compliant, though we hid such unworthy speculations behind a general attitude of soppy regard. It helped to know that our elders seemed to have got the hang of it, yet often I wondered where love showed up.

I was aware suddenly that Wallis was watching me, and without detachment. It was such an unusual state of affairs I lost composure and pretended to be deeply interested in the scene around me. A waiter was swerving in and out of the tables, holding aloft on the palm of one hand a great serving dish which glittered under the light; it was so heavy it spun him round and he swooped down and rose again like a juggler, at which I clapped my hands and shouted, 'Well caught, sir.' From the dais banked with palms came a

45

whine of strings and the tinkle of a piano as the ship's orchestra battled to be heard above the incessant sea-roar of conversation.

'Morgan,' said Wallis, and then fell silent, though she still looked at me.

'Yes,' I said, and waited. I did fancy, seeing she was hesitant, that she was about to make amends for having rebuked me so severely over that business of Kitty Webb's jewels. She wouldn't apologise, that wasn't her way, but she possibly intended to soften her words. After all, vulgar was a pretty strong denouncement of something only meant as a joke.

'That man,' she said, at last. 'Who is he?'

'I'm afraid I didn't ask,' I said, deflated. 'I merely laid him flat on the sidewalk, rang the bell of the nearest house and had the housekeeper send for a constable.'

'I wasn't–' she began.

'When he arrived, though only after some considerable time–'

'Morgan–' she interrupted.

'I explained I'd never seen him before in my life and went home.'

'I'm not talking about the dead man,' she said. 'I mean the one who–' but before she could enlighten me, Molly Dodge pushed back her chair and said she wanted to dance.

We walked in procession to the Palm Court. Young Melchett had crumbs caught in his yellow moustache. Wallis Ellery swayed at my side, swinging her white-gloved arms. When I opened the doors she rose on the toes of her white satin shoes.

The band hadn't yet arrived and Ginsberg and the other fellows went off to the adjoining smoke-room. They promised to return as soon as they heard the music. I might have followed them if Wallis hadn't chosen to sit next to me. It turned me giddy. For half an hour, at least, she scarcely spoke to Molly or Ida. Though I can't claim she hung on to my every word, she was remarkably civil and attentive. Molly kept rolling her eyes and smirking.

We talked about Sissy and the baby for a time. She thought Sissy terribly brave to go through all that sort of thing, though supposed it was worth it. And she rather liked Whitney.

'Sissy chose him for his eyelashes,' I told her.

'How sensible,' she said. 'They, at least, are sure to be genuine.'

I announced I was rather looking forward to having children, a thought that had never before crossed my mind. 'And I'll make sure they're properly looked after.'

'Yes,' she said. 'They should always be looked after, shouldn't they?... By someone or other.'

Sissy, who liked her, said her cleverness stemmed from conflict. Her father kept a string of 'girlies' and her mother had twice attempted suicide. Her last botched effort, when she'd flung herself from the first floor of their Boston town house, had resulted in a damaged spine and confinement to a wheel chair. I wasn't so sure cleverness arose from that sort of thing. In our circle such family upsets were commonplace, but then, so was stupidity.

She leaned nearer and looked into my eyes. It was all I could do to stop my lips from trembling. She wanted to know what I'd been doing in London for the past two months and why we hadn't run into one another. I explained I'd spent a deal of time with Melchett's people in Dorset, and for the rest I'd been occupied with family business.

'What sort of business?' she asked, as though she really cared. 'Surely you're not interested in banking, Morgan?'

It was very encouraging. In my head I mouthed, *Darling, you are my best girl*, though even as I was romancing, her eyes, brilliant as glass, were cutting through my dreams. I said I'd been sent over to supervise the transportation of my uncle's European art collection now that American import duties had been abolished. It wasn't quite the truth. Jack was in charge of that sort of thing, though I had signed papers on the Trust's behalf.

'You mean to tell me,' she cried, 'that all those wonderful Rubenses and Rembrandts are down in the hold this very moment?'

'No,' I said. 'There was a postponement due to the miners' strike. The shipment will follow later.'

'And will you come back again to keep an eye on things?'

I said I rather thought I wouldn't. There followed a dreary interlude in which she pressed me to explain what import duties entailed. I wasn't clear myself and tried to change the subject, mentioning I had been working for the previous year on the design of the *Titanic*, though leaving out my involvement with plumbing.

She seemed loath to drop the subject of my uncle's paintings, or rather the difficulties surrounding the consignment, which was both puzzling and disappointing. I had thought our conversation was developing rather differently and had even been getting up steam to suggest a stroll on deck.

'It's a fearful responsibility,' she said. 'being in charge of such valuable works of art.'

'Or would have been,' I said.

'But then, of course, you have your associates aboard.'

'What associates?' I said. 'I haven't any associates.'

'I thought I saw you with someone in the foyer ... earlier, before we anchored off Cherbourg.'

'I was with Melchett,' I told her. 'We made a tour of the lower decks. It was quite an experience. Perhaps tomorrow you'd like me to show you below. As a member of Mr Andrews' design team I can go anywhere I want.'

'Perhaps,' she said, without enthusiasm, and something, some illumination of the soul, died in her eyes and soon after she turned away and gave her attention to Molly Dodge.

Aggrieved, I took myself off to the smoke-room where I found Charlie Melchett making calculations on the back of an envelope. Ginsberg had come up with the idea of making a book on the time of our arrival in New York. Apparently the steerage passengers had rigged up a blackboard on the third class promenade down on the stern of C deck and were taking money quite openly.

'We can't lay bets,' said Hopper, 'till we've studied form. We have to know average speed and take weather conditions into consideration.'

'Twenty-four knots,' Charlie ventured, and was shouted down by Ginsberg who knew for a fact that we couldn't go beyond twenty-one or twenty-two. 'We haven't the coal to go full speed. I reckon we'll do no more than twenty, and that only if we've got the weather on our side.'

Someone tapped my shoulder; it was the fat man I had seen earlier in the company of Scurra and old Seefax. He said, without preamble, 'Where is she?'

'She?' I said.

'Is she with him?'

'Him?' I said.

His eyes were enormous, like an infant's, and lachrymose. There was a vacant chair against the wall and he pulled it forward and sat heavily down. I thought that showed cheek, but there was something in his expression, a mixture of hope and extreme resolve, that held me.

'I think you are a friend of his,' he said. 'I would like your opinion of him.' He had a curious accent which for no immediate reason I found familiar. His intonation was Jewish, of course, but his vowels were oddly flat.

I said, 'I haven't the least idea who you're talking about.'

'The man disfigured in a fencing duel.'

We stared at one another.

'The man with the dent in his mouth,' he urged, patting his lip with one podgy finger. 'The man with the gift of the gab.'

I almost smiled, it being such an apt description. All the same, I protested I scarcely knew Scurra and had only learnt his name that afternoon.

'But you have formed an opinion?' He actually seized my arm, which startled me.

'I can't help you,' I said.

'You must pay attention,' he urged. 'I have no time for subterfuge. I am a man of strong passions.'

'You surprise me,' I said, looking pointedly down at his hand.

He released me at once. 'I have made a mistake,' he muttered. 'You are, after all, too young to be curious.' Yet he still transfixed me with those moist and sentimental eyes.

'Morgan,' interrupted Ginsberg, a glass in either hand, 'I gather the purser's the fellow to ask about average speeds. What say you and I go in search of him?'

I rose immediately and followed him into the revolving doors which spun us out into the foyer. From the Palm Court came the strains of jazz-time.

He said, 'You seemed to be having trouble with our stout friend, Rosenfelder.'

'You know him?'

'Scurra introduced me.'

'You know Scurra?'

'Don't you?'

'Yes, of course,' I said, and left it at that. For a man who continually played the fool he was remarkably astute, from which I concluded he was not quite straight. I'm capable of making such a judgement, being often not entirely straight myself.

The information we wanted, the purser told us, would be available tomorrow, once we had left Queenstown. He agreed with Ginsberg that they wouldn't be pushing the ship this trip. 'Perhaps 500 miles a day,' he estimated. 'Maybe more, maybe less.'

'But you reckon we'll reach New York Tuesday?' pressed

51

Ginsberg, and the purser replied, 'Tuesday night, yes. Barring accidents,' at which they both laughed.

The office was cosy from the warmth of an electric fire. Above the desk was pinned a photograph of an infant scowling beneath the shadow of a summer bonnet. 'A fine little chap,' Ginsberg remarked. 'What do you call him?' Assuming a sugary expression he touched the child's paper jowls with the tip of one finger.

'Eliza,' said the purser. 'After her mother.'

Remembering I hadn't a receipt for the luggage transported by Melchett's chauffeur, I enquired if it was to hand. After much rifling through the compartments of his desk the purser produced the relevant docket. 'One medium sized trunk,' he read, 'and a consignment of theatrical manuscripts in the name of J. Pierpont Morgan.'

We were about to leave when Ginsberg said, 'I noticed when looking out of the saloon windows that while the sea and the skyline were evident on my left, only the sky was visible to starboard. From which I gained the impression we've a distinct list to port.'

'Very well observed, sir,' exclaimed the purser. 'It's no doubt due to more coal being consumed from the starboard bunkers than from the port side.'

'Which is occasioned, no doubt,' said Ginsberg, 'by the fire blazing in the stokehold of Number 10 bunker.'

The purser looked shaken. 'A fire, sir? What do you mean?'

'Come now. We both know what I'm talking about.'

'A fire?' I reiterated, stupidly enough. 'What sort of fire?'

'The sort that burns,' retorted Ginsberg.

'If what you imply was true, sir,' the purser said, 'the Board of Trade inspector would never have signed the clearance certificate for us to leave Southampton.'

'Well then,' cried Ginsberg, 'we have nothing to worry about, have we?'

'What was all that about?' I asked, when we were in the corridor. He replied that he was a cautious man, which struck me as absurd, and that he had always found it inadvisable to take anything on trust.

I didn't return with him to the smoke-room; his know-all attitude irritated me. Sissy has constantly warned that my intolerance will land me in hot water. I've always felt that if a man tries to adopt attitudes which are not innate then sooner or later he will discover Nature cannot be forced. We are what we are, and it's no good dissembling.

Pleading lack of sleep and a mild queasiness of stomach, I loitered outside the Palm Court and listened to the band. A vocalist was singing *Put your arms around me honey, hold me tight*. Peering through the glass panels of the doors I caught sight of Rosenfelder, coat-tails flying as he strutted Molly Dodge across the floor. There was no sign of Wallis Ellery.

Before retiring I went out on to the boat deck. There was a breeze but the air was far from cold. An elderly couple sat on steamer chairs, hands folded on their laps. From somewhere ahead came the squeal of bagpipes; walking astern I joined a group of passengers who stood at the rails looking on to the steerage space beneath. They were dancing down there, a kind of skirl, the men whooping as they swept the women in figures of eight about the deck. Someone next to me murmured, 'They know how to enjoy themselves,' and another said, 'How steady the ship is,' to which her companion replied, as though quoting from the brochures, 'We're on a floating palace, my dear.'

Standing there, watching a woman who stood with her back to the crowd, shawl draped about her head and shoulders, I fancied I half remembered my own steerage passage to the New World, though indeed I didn't, having only learnt of it from my aunt. She said I'd been put in the care of an Irish girl who reported I ate enough for three and was never sick. It was not meanness, I was assured, that had governed the decision to transport me so cheaply across the Atlantic, rather that it was felt more exalted accommodation, bearing in mind the circumstances of my early years, would have caused almost as much embarrassment to myself as to others. Sissy, of course, says it was because my aunt did not want people to know of our connection, but then, as she has never been abandoned, Sissy can afford to be critical.

The figure in the shawl turned and, circling the dancers, came to the metal gate barring the way to the second class area. She stood leaning against it, peering upwards, and with the light full on her face I recognised who she was. I was astonished. It was hardly likely that anyone travelling first or second class would choose to visit the lower decks and it was strictly against the rules for steerage passengers to move upwards, and yet I had seen her twice in first class, once in the company of Scurra when we left Southampton and again when she had appeared on the Grand Staircase and called out to him.

Presently a fellow with a handkerchief knotted about his throat approached. He spoke to the woman but she shrugged her shoulders dismissively and fixed her gaze on the heavens. Save for the mast lights sailing against the darkness the sky was empty of stars.

Puzzled, I strolled back the way I had come and reaching the gymnasium doors stood for some minutes leaning over the rail. The ship was lit up from bow to stern, the reflections leaping in silver streamers across the black waters below. I could feel the coldness of the rail striking through the cloth of my jacket, and as I shifted my arm an image of the corridor at Princes Gate flashed into my head; I clearly saw my elbow bobbing upward to wipe away that square of dust on the wall. My heart leapt in my breast and I found it difficult to breathe. It was only a matter of time, I reasoned, before Jack or one of the servants noticed the empty space.

It wasn't being found out that bothered me – my uncle was three-quarters buccaneer himself – more that my aunt had dinned into me that wrong-doing is invariably punished, and though my adult self regarded this as mere superstition the child in me quaked. I exaggerate, of course. There was definitely something pleasurable in my moment of fear. I decided I would write to my uncle, confessing what I had done. I might even offer to pay for the painting – my allowance was generous enough.

When I passed through the gymnasium there were some fellows fooling about on the apparatus. The instructor, poor chap, was trying to close up for the night. I nearly stopped to assist him – the revellers were distinctly the worse for drink – but decided against it. I suspected I might well be in the same condition in the nights that followed.

I rang for the steward on reaching my stateroom. I wanted a hot drink. He came in at once, carrying the day suit I had worn when boarding. He said it had been sponged and pressed. The contents of the pockets were on the dressing table if I cared to check.

'Is there a Jew called Rosenfelder on this deck?' I asked.

'Not on this one, sir. He's on B deck. He's the gentleman I mentioned who was to have travelled second class and took over a cancellation.'

'And what of a man called Scurra?'

'That name I don't recollect, sir. Possibly he's travelling under an assumed name. You'd be surprised how many of them do that.'

'Like Mr and Mrs Morgan,' I suggested, and he knew immediately who I meant. He had served them for years on the Atlantic run and found his Lordship a very affable man. He didn't lean much towards her Ladyship, whom he found strident. 'Of course, she's an American,' he said, 'and they're never backward in coming forward.' He had met her sort before, when he was young and employed as a ball-room dancer at the Savoy. In those days two dances were included in the price of the tea, for the benefit of the unac-companied ladies. Though he wasn't one to blow his own trumpet he had been a great favourite with those leaving the glades of youth.

'One in particular,' he boasted, 'took a fancy to me. She used to collect me in her carriage and we'd spank along to the Park and take a wee drop of gin under the trees. Mind, I never took advantage … I left that to her.'

Her Ladyship's sister went under the name of Elinor Glyn. She wrote novels, of the steamy sort so he'd heard, and was, or had been, the mistress of Lord Curzon. I didn't rebuke him for gossiping, thinking he might be useful later.

Giving him his tip I suddenly remembered the seaman who had taken Melchett and myself down to the engine rooms. Putting a half-crown piece in an envelope, I addressed it to Riley. I told the steward to make sure the right man received it. 'He's no bigger than a boy,' I said. 'And he talks like a foreigner with a cold.'

My billfold, matches, the keys to Princes Gate and the snapshot foisted on me by the dying man lay on the dressing table. I stuffed them back into the pocket of the jacket and began my letter. *My dear Uncle, I am bringing back with me the small painting of my mother, dated 1888, which hung on the first floor corridor at Princes Gate. I did not have time to tell Jack what –.*

I had got no further when my cocoa arrived. Laying the letter aside I prepared for bed. It was a relief to switch off the light because the girl on the wall now seemed to be watching me.

TWO

Thursday, 11th April

At seven o'clock the next morning I had the salt water baths to myself and had swum eight lengths in less than five minutes without pausing for rest. On my ninth turn, a corpulent figure emerged from the cubicles and padded towards the side. I was put off my stroke; it was none other than Rosenfelder, dressed in a costume of green and brown stripes, his calves white and shapely as a girl's. He sat for some minutes on the edge of the pool struggling to thrust his curls into a rubber cap before flopping walrus-fashion into the water. Though disconcerted I was damned if I was going to quit on his account and continued to plough back and forth, until, having blindly thrashed into my path, his arm flailed downwards and struck me on the shoulder.

We both trod water and faced each other, he spluttering apologies, myself gasping for breath from lack of fitness. I was about to respond impatiently when his bathing cap, which was already absurdly balanced like some deflating balloon on the very top of his head, suddenly rose in the air and plopped down between us. The sight was so comical I bellowed with laughter. He stared at me a second, eyes popping, and then he too began to squeal. We both clung to one another for support and were not much better composed when we climbed out, for the floor was slippery from our splashings and we were forced to walk on mincing tip-toe to avoid falling, which set us off again, our guffaws bouncing back at us from the tiled walls as we pranced to the changing boxes. We continued to behave in this cocka-mamie fashion while dressing, he giving vent to falsetto giggles, myself letting out staccato hoots as I towelled my-self dry.

He suggested we breakfasted together, which was fine by me. I found him amusing. By the time I had tucked into my eggs, bacon and kidneys and he into his kedgeree, we were the best of friends.

After the politenesses had been rushed through, the weather, the size of the ship, the excellence of the food, he was eager to talk about himself. At some point in his unstop-pable narrative Thomas Andrews and four of his design team entered the restaurant. They each carried drawing pads and Andrews had a pencil stuck behind his ear. He didn't notice me.

Rosenfelder's story was commonplace enough for one of his race and class. He had left Germany as a boy and come to England to be apprenticed to a tailor, an elderly cousin on his father's side. They had lived first in Liverpool and then Manchester.

'They were not good times,' he confided. 'My cousin was a hard man … life had made him so. Blows in the shop, blows in the home … never enough to eat, bugs crawling out of the skirting boards and always the rain coming down.'

'I can imagine,' I said. And I could. I rubbed my arm to relieve an itch.

'Bit by bit the business began to prosper. My cousin had the customers and I had the skill at cutting. We make money. Then, when my cousin popped his clogs … you understand the expression?' – I nodded – 'he left me five sewing machines, a quantity of cloth and a year's rent on the premises of the top floor of a warehouse in Hood Street beside the canal. Modest, you understand, but the roof didn't leak.'

'It's a river,' I interrupted. 'The Irwell.'

'I'd been frugal,' he continued, 'and in another year I'd saved enough to take a lease on a shop in a better part of town. Twelve months later, after a courtship of fifteen years, I marry the daughter of a Russian pastry cook employed in the Midland Hotel. She's a good woman, thrifty, a regular *baleboosteh*. When we have our first child she loses her teeth. Now, when she moves her mouth to speak to me, which is fortunately not often, I am regretfully reminded of a goldfish.' He had bought her dentures, of course, the best that money could buy, but she refused to wear them.

Lest I should think the tailoring business lacked poetry he dazzled me with a recitation of fabrics – bombazine, brocade, calico, dimity, duck, flannelette, fustian, muslin, sateen, velveteen. He was going to America to see Mr Macy and show him an extraordinary dress which would, God willing, go on display in the windows of that famous store and eventually make him his fortune. 'I will be,' he declared, 'no longer a bespoke tailor but a couturier.'

'Mr Macy,' I told him, 'is on board. Or rather the present owner of the store. His name is Isador Straus.'

'Here? On this ship?' He fairly gawped at me.

'He's an elderly gentleman with a beard, travelling with his wife.'

'You think I should speak to him?'

'Possibly,' I said. 'If you choose your moment. He's a good man, a philanthropist. Like you, he started with nothing.'

And then, because I was curious, though indeed he had accused me only the night before of not being old enough, I mentioned the tall woman in the South Western Hotel. 'Forgive me,' I said, 'but I couldn't help noticing the way you looked at her.'

'Ah,' he breathed, and crumbled the toast on his plate. For once, he was at a loss for words.

'It was my impression,' I prompted, 'that you were sweet on her.'

'I had never set eyes on her before in my life,' he said, and launched into an explanation concerning the contents of the oblong box I had seen him so zealously guarding, namely a garment which, on account of it being designed for a window display, had been cut larger than life and doomed merely to drape the celluloid contours of a shop dummy. That is, until the woman in the hotel got up to leave.

'She rose like a tree,' he cried. 'An English oak. It could have been made for her.'

I said, 'I thought it was desire you felt.'

'And so it was,' he insisted. 'The desire to see my dress on a creature of flesh and blood.'

I brought up Scurra's name. In Rosenfelder's opinion he was an educated man with a near spiritual grasp of human nature. 'Do you know what he told me? Listen – *one day the*

64

world will recognise the tailor as the hierophant and hierarch, even its God. I look in the dictionary, you understand, to make him out.'

'One would need to,' I said. 'I take it you know him well?'

'Not at all. I observed him talking to the tall goddess and I think to myself, here is a man to confide in.'

'And did you?'

'But, of course. He advises me not to approach her until after we have left Queenstown. She was to have met a gentleman friend at Southampton. He did not show up. He is her protector, if you follow me. Nor did he appear at Cherbourg, at which she becomes so distraught she threatens to throw herself overboard. Scurra has persuaded her to wait until we reach Queenstown. Her friend may yet turn up. She has left London with her ticket, the clothes she stands up in, a small suitcase and two pounds in her purse.'

'How very unfortunate,' I said.

'For her, yes. For me, who knows what will be the advantage?'

'Has Scurra known her long?'

'That's for him to say.'

I would quite happily have passed the morning with him if he hadn't had an appointment with the barber; there was a miracle lotion advertised, guaranteed to straighten ringlets.

I spent two hours in the library, wrestling to compose another letter to my uncle. I had first tried the writing room – it had a stock of paper embossed with the White Star crest – but found it full of women, including Molly Dodge. She said I'd been a disappointment to her last night, sloping off

65

like that. I didn't have to lie to Molly so I confided I'd felt blue.

'You missed the fun,' she said.

'I'm tired of fun.'

'If I didn't know you better,' she replied, 'I'd think you were playing a part.'

I got no further with my letter than I had the night before. It now struck me as unnecessary to tell my uncle about my mother's picture. Beyond suggesting I might have told Jack what I'd done, I doubted he'd give a button. After all, he had enough paintings to fill the Louvre and though irascible was neither grasping nor censorious. He hadn't the need. Unlike his millionaire associates on Wall Street he'd inherited wealth, not clawed his way up from poverty. It was power that motivated him rather than money, and a belief that he alone could set America straight.

I reckon I was, still am, ambivalent towards my uncle. It would have helped my cause if he had been more of a rogue. True, he was a hypocrite, not least in his shenanigans with women – he had once put a stop to a production of *Salomé* at the Metropolitan Opera House, on the grounds that the reasons for chopping off the Baptist's head were downright salacious – but then, he knew he was. A cynic, he was fond of quoting the maxim that a man has two reasons for the things he does, a good one and the real one.

What was more urgent, I realised, as I lolled yawning over the library table, was to figure out a way to tell him what I intended to do with my future. Since I was nineteen my uncle had been trying to fix me up with employment. How often had I heard him thunder that it was the duty of the wealthy to work? A poor man without a job, he held, was less despicable than a rich man who remained idle.

Under pressure I had undergone six months in a merchant bank in Paris, a miserable three weeks in a backwater branch of the Union Pacific Railroad Company, a year in the library run by his one-time secretary and mistress, Bella da Costa Greene, and a further year in the offices of Harland and Wolff. That last momentous year had propelled me towards the crossroads of my life and shown me the path I must take. Unfortunately for my uncle, it led more towards destruction than construction and had nothing whatever to do with draughtsmanship or naval architecture.

It wasn't the financing of my plans that bothered me. Even if my uncle stopped my allowance, which wasn't likely, my aunt had money of her own and would chuck me the moon if I asked. It was my conscience that niggled, for I'd been treated with great generosity by one who owed me nothing. We were linked by events, not blood, and he viewed me as if through a microscope, the *infusoria* of his long-gone past wriggling before his magnified gaze.

I was about to doze off when Hopper and Melchett swept in and dragged me away to the gymnasium. Colonel Astor was there, morose as ever, sitting in the row-boat machine, clad in a white singlet. The boxing gloves were missing but we took turns, bare-knuckled, at the punch-bag. Hopper was terrific at it, taking almighty swings and ending up scarcely puffed. Every time Melchett made a hit he cried out 'Ouch' and ran about with his hand tucked under his armpit. Astor never looked up.

Just after noon we tumbled out on deck. The sun shone

so brilliantly that a small boy standing only five yards distant dissolved into whiteness, the top he was whipping gyrating at the toes of his all but invisible boots.

Slowly we approached Queenstown, the green fields spreading back from the cliffs. In time I could make out the glint of windows beyond the harbour wall, the white moon of a municipal clock. On Spy Hill a church spire speared the mild sky. Tethered to the quay, bobbing like apples, two squat tugs rode the water. Presently, the screws churning up brown sand, we stopped engines and waited for the pilot to come out.

I thought of the day, three months after my arrival in Belfast, when I'd met Tuohy on my way to the draughts-men's huts. It was raining and I'd taken a short cut through the alleyway on Harland Road. It was springtime and the pussy-willows were coming into bud. Ahead of me strode a working man with his tucker box under his arm. All of a sudden he staggered and fell down. Men were often laid off because they'd taken alcohol before the dawn shift, and I thought he was drunk. I would have side-stepped him if his box hadn't burst open, spilling two slices of bread into my path. I couldn't bring myself to tread them into the puddles. Looking down I saw the man was white as milk and there was froth bubbling at the corner of his bloodless lips. Kneeling, I shook him and after a moment he recovered and struggled upright. He said he'd had a fit, which was not uncommon to him, and asked me not to tell his foreman. He didn't beg me to keep silent or wheedle in any way; indeed, he spoke to me as if we were equals. 'My name is Tuohy,' he said and shook my hand. Taken aback by his authoritative

68

manner, and as he remained the colour of chalk and none too steady on his feet, I offered him my arm. I remember fretting about his dinner bread soaking up the wet. Three weeks later I attended my first meeting. The following month I visited his home.

That first time I had been foolish enough to think it would be me who would put his family at their ease. I took his mother flowers; she received them without a word, but her eyes flashed contempt. She wore a man's cap on her head and men's boots on her feet.

At half-past twelve two tenders ploughed towards the *Titanic*, bringing out mail and passengers. Bearing in mind Rosenfelder's woman, I was about to walk astern to look down on the steerage space when a commotion broke out further along the deck. Following the crowd who were now flowing in that direction and coming within view of the dummy funnel which served as a ventilation outlet, I saw a black face emerging from the top. It was only a stoker who had climbed up as some sort of practical joke, or possibly for a bet, but several silly women, including Mrs Brown of Denver, taking it for an apparition shot up from the very flames of hell, screamed in alarm and declared it an omen.

An hour later the engines started again and we turned a quarter-circle to point along the coast, the pigmy ships in the harbour hooting our departure. The fellow with the bagpipes was standing on the poop blowing a melancholy farewell to old Erin. I don't doubt the ghastly wailing of his instrument was construed by the women as yet another omen.

The ship was followed by a storm cloud of gulls drawn by the remains of lunch pouring out of the waste pipes. Hopper, with hopes of slinging them out of the sky, tried to borrow the small boy's whip. Snatching up his top the child ran squealing for his mother. Hopper roamed off in search of a long pole and didn't return.

All afternoon we steamed along the coast, the sea-birds still dipping and screaming in our wake, the green hills and fields fading to grey as the light began to seep from the day. Melchett and I stayed on deck until dusk, until the coast curved away to the north-west and the last mountains melted into darkness.

*

At seven o'clock that evening, as arranged, I met Charlie Melchett in the main lounge for a drink before dinner. Earlier, we'd agreed to dine in the à la carte restaurant so as to avoid Ginsberg. Melchett didn't like him. He agreed Ginsberg was cleverer than he let on but reckoned he'd a malicious streak. He said it was all right for the likes of Hopper to be friendly with him – as he was equally cynical no harm could be done – but by and large it didn't do for less sophisticated men to be exposed to that kind of influence. I was touched by his erroneous view of my character. As it happened, I didn't care where I dined just as long as I didn't have to sit at the same table with teasing Wallis Ellery.

Melchett had been cornered by Lady Duff Gordon, who greeted me by name and claimed she'd been looking for me since breakfast. She spoke with eyes lowered and head tilted to one side, addressing my shirt front. 'I'm having a small dinner party this evening and would adore you to be present. Eight o'clock sharp. I've invited your friend Van Hopper, and Charlie, of course, so do say you'll come.'

'It's very kind of you,' I began, but before I could add another word she had turned away, one hand fluttering the air to attract the attention of a new arrival.

'She's nicer than she seems,' Melchett said, reading my expression. 'And she's not idle. She runs a very successful business … as a couturier.'

'I doubt I can wait until eight o'clock,' I protested. 'We did without luncheon, don't forget.'

I felt a little less irritable after my second glass of champagne and experienced only a slight stab of despair at the entrance of Wallis and her sister Ida. I was lucky, I consoled myself, not to know the constraints of requited love. Love, I reasoned, stripped a man to the bone. After which thought I got to my feet and sought out Lady Duff Gordon. She was in the company of a buffoon with an eyeglass who was guffawing so loudly I had to bellow to make myself heard.

'Forgive me,' I said, 'but I promised to dine with a friend, a Mr Rosenfelder. I'm afraid I can't break the arrangement.'

She responded as I had expected, 'Then I insist you bring him with you.'

When I returned to Melchett he was swivelled round in his chair, staring in the direction of the foyer doors. I was in time to see Wallis leaving on the arm of Scurra.

'Who is that man?' Melchett asked. 'He seems to know everyone on board.'

'To hell with him,' I growled. 'To hell with all of them.' I was hungry enough to eat a horse and my upper arms were hurting like the devil from my exercise at the punch-bag. Melchett, looking concerned, attempted to jolly me up.

'I met a man this tea-time who used to know you at St Mark's. I didn't catch his name. He works in his father's business in Boston ... something to do with dry goods. Tall and clean-shaven. Rather shy in manner ... not the pushy sort ... would you know who I mean?'

'No,' I snapped. In that floating room whose mirrored walls duplicated the crowd milling back and forth beneath the trembling chandeliers, the familiar, similar reflections raced like demons across the embellished glass.

'He said you were frightfully good on the tennis courts and had once lent him money when he was in a jam.'

'For God's sake,' I burst out. 'The world consists of men who know us. Look around you. This place is chock-a-block with people who went to the same schools, the same universities, attended the same fencing classes, shared the same dancing masters, music teachers, Latin tutors, tennis coaches–'

'Morgan,' Melchett said. 'You're shouting.'

'I could pick out fifty or more I've known half my life and Lord knows how many others I've shared a dinner table with in half the capitals of Europe. There isn't a photograph taken from here to the Nile that doesn't feature twenty or more of us lined up to watch the dicky-bird.'

'If you say so,' he murmured, hoping to calm me.

'Why, half the older men here have even shared the same mistresses.'

'Steady on,' he hissed.

'One big unhappy family,' I concluded gloomily, and got up and left. I guess poor old Charlie was relieved.

Once in the foyer I sped up the stairs and out on to the deck. Here I walked furiously up and down, muttering aloud, taking the part of both prosecution and defence. I can't recall what case I was arguing, beyond it had something to do with the transparency of men and the inscrutability of women, but I reckon I must have sounded fairly unhinged.

I was on the point of returning to make my peace with Melchett when I heard a peculiar cry, high and fierce like a cat caught by the tail. It came from the shadows cast by the overhang of a life-boat. Then I heard Scurra's unmistakable voice. He was tussling with someone reclining in a steamer chair. For a wild moment I feared it might be Wallis, then he dodged to one side to avoid an outflung hand and I saw it was Rosenfelder's woman.

'Her friend didn't board at Queenstown,' I said.

'It would seem not,' he replied breathlessly.

At that instant the woman got the better of him and leaping to her feet made a dash for the rail, yowling horribly. Scurra and I fled in pursuit and succeeded in seizing her by either arm. He and I were both a little under six foot in height yet she towered above us. Wrestling to restrain her I couldn't help thinking we resembled those tugs at Southampton endeavouring to drag the *Titanic* out of the path of the SS *New York*.

'Have you a cabin on B deck?' Scurra panted, the woman

thrashing back and forth in our grip like a tree caught in the wind.

'I'm a deck below.'

'Fetch Rosenfelder,' he ordered, and I let go of the woman and scooted towards the gymnasium. No sooner had I hurled myself through the doors than I collided with Thomas Andrews.

He said, 'There appears to be some fault with four of the dormitory bath taps in E accommodation.'

'It will be the washers,' I replied and raced on.

Rosenfelder wasn't in the saloon or either of the restaurants. Nor was he to be found in the Café Parisien. Wallis was there. She called out to me but I ignored her; it gave me pleasure.

I ran Rosenfelder to earth in the smoke-room, playing cards in pretty unsavoury company. I said, 'Come with me. It's urgent.'

'I'll be along presently.'

I went so far as to tug at his sleeve. He was holding the cards close to his chest, a foolish indication that he'd been dealt a good hand.

'He didn't board at Queenstown,' I hissed, which did the trick. He rose instantly, still clutching his cards, and followed me from the room.

When we arrived on deck it was to see Scurra on his knees, clinging to the woman's ankle. She was dragging him behind her.

'Aie, yi, yi,' wailed Rosenfelder.

I'm ashamed to say I giggled.

Between us we coaxed her indoors. Mercifully she'd gone

74

quiet, and beyond a few curious glances in the foyer and the kindly interference of a steward who enquired if the lady was in need of the ship's doctor, we got her safely to Rosenfelder's stateroom. Here Scurra guided her towards the bedroom but Rosenfelder insisted on the sofa in the sitting room, out of delicacy I supposed. Having made sure her head was comfortably supported on a cushion he lit a cigar and stood at the dressing table, smoothing down his hair with a silver-backed brush. He patted the cards stuffed into his top pocket. 'Such a good hand,' he sighed.

'Are you sure she doesn't need a doctor?' I asked.

'And what would he tell us?' said Scurra. 'Everything is already diagnosed. It's simply that we can't see the whole picture.' Taking off his jacket and hanging it carelessly on the edge of a painting screwed to the wall, he retired to the bathroom to clean himself up.

The woman lay perfectly still, eyes closed, feet propped up on the arm of the sofa. She was dressed as I had seen her in the hotel. From my perch on the stool beside the writing desk I could see the soles of her shoes were worn into holes. Puffing on his Havana Rosenfelder switched on the electric fire and circling the sofa sank cross-legged to the floor, gazing intently into the woman's smoke wreathed face. He wore a beatific smile and looked like a Buddha. Neither of us spoke; we were both waiting for Scurra to return and give us instructions.

I studied the painting, of which only a corner was to be seen, the rest obscured by the folds of Scurra's coat. I made out a scarlet brush stroke and reckoned it was a flower, possibly a detail in some pastoral landscape. It was very quiet, save for Rosenfelder inhaling on his cigar and the faint thrum of the engines far below us.

Presently Scurra came out of the bathroom and dusted down his trouser knees with the silver-backed brush. His hair stood up in damp tufts and he was beaming. 'Good boy,' he said, turning to me and squeezing my arm. 'Good boy. You behaved very well.' I blushed quite as fully as Melchett. He had such an extraordinary warmth of manner that it was like lying in sunshine. You have to understand that the sort of men I mixed with, unless they were decadent types, kept each other at a distance, however involved by events or kinship. It wasn't that I thought of Scurra as a father figure or looked up to him – how could I, seeing I scarcely knew him – simply that in his presence it was possible to attach the word love to what one felt, and not wriggle at its implications. All the same, I went on blushing. When he retrieved his coat I saw that what I had taken to be the petal of a flower was in fact a splash of blood on a canvas depicting the bloodiest of battles. Later I was to remember that moment; I had mistaken a part for the whole.

'What do we do now?' I asked. 'Shouldn't we wake her?'

'She's not asleep,' said Scurra. 'She's composing herself, don't you think?'

So we waited, Scurra attending to his toilette and Rosenfelder reducing his cigar to a wet stub. The top buttons of the woman's coat had been torn off in the struggle on deck, exposing the dress beneath. I glimpsed her white throat and watched the bodice of her gown as it rose and fell. Though I was happy to be in Scurra's company I was beginning to wonder if I would ever eat again, and tortured myself with an image of a breast of duck dolloped with sweet apple.

'Rosenfelder,' I whispered. 'We have an engagement for dinner tonight with Lady Duff Gordon.'

'Me? I have not heard of such a woman.'

'She's travelling under an assumed name,' said Scurra. 'She's a couturier. It could be useful for you to know her.'

Rosenfelder looked impressed, but not unduly so. His attention lay entirely with the woman.

It seemed an age before she opened her eyes; when she did so she appeared neither startled nor embarrassed. 'A little brandy, perhaps?' suggested Scurra, and Rosenfelder bounded to his feet and opening a three-cornered cabinet fetched decanter and glasses. Pouring a generous measure he handed it to her. I could have done with a drink myself, if only to quieten the rumblings of my empty stomach, but he thought only of her. She sipped, gave a little cough, swung her feet gracefully to the floor and sat bolt upright. She was still beautiful in spite of her red-rimmed eyes and even more so when she took off her hat, for her hair was amber rather than gold, though that may have been the reflection of the fire.

She took things very calmly for one who had caused so much trouble. She didn't apologise though she expressed gratitude for the concern we had shown. Her voice was cultured, resonant. For all her threadbare shoes she was very much the lady.

'Doubtless you know my story,' she said. 'It's not uncommon and of little interest, except to myself.' Even so, she proceeded to tell it in some detail. Her name was Adele

77

Baines and she had been born of a French mother and English father under the Opera House in Paris. She had sung in the courtyard when hanging out the washing. At the age of twelve no less a personage than Madame Adiny had offered to train her voice. At nineteen she had come to London, and, unable to find work as a chanteuse, sought employment as a model at Fenwick's in Bond Street.

'God is telling me something,' exclaimed Rosenfelder.

After three years she had caught the eye of a director of the firm – he was married, naturally – and they had become lovers. She had accepted the nice meals in expensive restaurants and there had been three or four weekends at an hotel in Dieppe, but when he had wanted to set her up in an apartment in Manchester Square she had refused. She preferred her own room above a butcher's shop in Somers Town. It gave her independence. Then something happened, something that changed everything – Here she broke off and staring down at her left hand gave a little mew of annoyance.

'My nail,' she said, 'I've broken my nail.'

'The something,' Rosenfelder demanded. 'What is this something?'

Frowning, she continued.

The man's small son had fallen sick and almost died. She had made no demands and was always there when he needed her. For many nights she waited, with his permission, outside the hospital to comfort him when he stumbled out, the tears still wet on his cheeks. When the child was better they discovered that what had begun as merely an affair of passion had turned into true love. Two months ago he had arranged to take her to New York and introduce her to a man who had business connections with the Metropolitan Opera House. He had bought her a ticket, steerage passage so as to avoid scandal, and was to have joined her at Southampton. 'The rest you know,' she said. 'And have taken part in.'

It seemed to me that her speech had been well rehearsed. Truth to tell, my sympathies were with her vanished lover. When a woman declares she has made no demands one can be sure she believes she's owed something. I wanted to ask what on earth she'd been doing roaming about on the upper decks, but held my tongue. It might have sounded as if I thought she should have chosen to jump from a third class rail rather than a first.

Rosenfelder's face was wreathed in smiles. From the way he looked at her he was already taking measurements. Embarrassed, mostly on my own account, I said, 'It is most distressing for you, but hardly worth dying for.'

'Few things are,' observed Scurra, and laughed heartily. To my astonishment she joined in, though whether it was to keep him sweet or because she was hysterical I couldn't judge. He seemed to think she was in her right mind, for he offered to escort her back to E deck. Foolishly, I blurted out that it would look pretty rum if one of the stewards saw him with a steerage passenger.

'What an extraordinary chap you are,' he said. 'What does it matter what anyone thinks?'

I was mortified at having let myself down. I wanted his approval even more than my dinner and became wretchedly unctuous, offering my assistance to the woman, boasting of my connections, my influence aboard ship. When I'd finished making a show of myself she thanked me, the way one thanks a small child who offers to shoulder a bag it can scarcely lift. Rosenfelder, meantime, had fetched needle and thread and sewn her coat together. He addressed her as Adele and promised that in the morning he would find her some buttons. Then she covered that glorious hair with her hat and went off with Scurra.

We were late sitting down at the Duff Gordons' table. Rosenfelder was all for grovelling until I explained it wasn't good form to apologise. The Carters and Bruce Ismay were there, together with an English journalist called Stead who appeared to command respect. At President Taft's invitation he was on his way to make the closing speech at a convention bent on inducing businessmen to take an active part in religious movements.

'Great God,' murmured Ismay when he caught Stead's drift.

I knew how he felt. My uncle was a regular, even fanatical church-goer, as were most of his associates on Wall Street, and they too would have considered it sacrilege to mix scripture with commerce.

I began to enjoy myself, which I hadn't expected. I found Lady Duff Gordon entertaining – I soon forgot to call her Mrs Morgan – and forthright to an extent that might have passed for coarseness in a younger woman. She had a long thin face and a haughty expression, but that was just her style. Almost the instant I sat down she said she was glad to see I hadn't inherited the Morgan nose. I couldn't see any point in telling her there was no reason I should have;

instead I dwelt on the trouble my uncle's notable facial protuberance had caused him in his younger days, meaning he'd suffered agonies of self-consciousness over its size.

'It's not the only protuberance that's given him trouble,' she dryly remarked.

She was extremely good at dealing with people. Twice she adroitly punctured one of Ismay's more impatient utterances, without being offensive. And she took a positive shine to Rosenfelder, which endeared her to me. He, poor fellow, though delighted, perspired copiously under her attentions. He was having no luck with the barber's miracle lotion, his hair curling more wantonly by the minute.

'I am head of the dress firm of Madame Lucile,' she told him. 'You may have heard of it. You must come and visit me in New York.'

'Mrs Duff,' I heard him reply, evidently confused by the multiplicity of her names. 'That I should be given such an opportunity!'

I spent five minutes engaged in a stilted exchange with Bruce Ismay, whom I knew quite well and didn't care for. Unlike most Englishmen, he lacked apathy. He asked me if I had enjoyed my time at Harland and Wolff.

'Yes, indeed,' I said. He had put the same question many times before and received the same answer. I asked him whether he thought we were going to break any records on our maiden voyage, and he replied something to the effect that heads would roll if we damn well didn't.

Outwardly he appeared confident, harsh almost, a demeanour which many held to be a deceptive covering developed to protect the sensitive man beneath. In my opinion this was so much baloney. He did have layers, but like an onion they were all the same. Now chief executive of the White Star Line, he had once owned it. My uncle, determined to dominate the transatlantic route, had made him an offer he couldn't refuse; though the company had made huge earnings from Boer War contracts, my uncle coughed up ten times its value.

Some years before, on a visit to England, I'd spent a weekend in Ismay's company and not forgotten it. We were both guests of Sanderson, his fellow director, who had a house in Freshfield in Lancashire. Sanderson was captain of the county golf club and his house was built among pine woods swarming with red squirrels. His butler lent us guns and we spent a whole morning blasting them to bits from the porch. Even in high summer the wind blew and I emptied my shoes of sand a dozen times a day. Beyond the trees lay the black edge of the Irish Sea.

The night of our arrival Mrs Sanderson gave a large dinner party, in my honour as much as Ismay's. My connections have always made me welcome and the cotton merchants and shipping owners who attended treated me very civilly. At the end of the meal and before the women had left the room Mr Sanderson got up to make a little speech of welcome. It wasn't a strictly formal occasion – there'd even been a bit of tomfoolery between the pudding and cheese involving the chucking of golf balls into the fruit bowl. I was seated to the left of Sanderson, next to a lady with a pug dog on her lap, Ismay on his right. I took out my cigarettes – the other men were already smoking – and being without matches reached across to bring the candles nearer, at which Ismay, leaning out over the table, violently slapped my outstretched hand. I was not yet eighteen years old.

Smarting still, I wondered what he would say if I brought up that distant incident, and might have done if I hadn't caught Melchett's eye. He was looking distinctly frosty. I couldn't think what was the matter with him until I suddenly remembered I'd walked out on him earlier.

'Charlie,' I pleaded, filled with genuine remorse. 'Forgive me, there's a good fellow. I was out of sorts.'

Good fellow that he was, he responded instantly, even to getting to his feet and coming to shake me by the hand.

At the end of the table Mrs Carter was shuddering in mock horror. Apparently the journalist Stead had once written a short story about a ship hit by an iceberg which she claimed to have read.

'I can't remember the ending,' she cried, 'but I know I had nightmares for weeks.'

'Mr Stead ought to write one about a stoker coming up out a funnel,' said Hopper. 'Although the ladies have pretty well written it already.'

'What did happen at the end?' shouted Lady Duff Gordon. I noticed she had her hand on Rosenfelder's arm.

'They all drowned,' said Stead. 'All but the Captain.'

'You shouldn't let Wallis upset you,' whispered Melchett. 'She's not worth it,' which nearly put me out of sorts all over again.

The party broke up at about eleven o'clock, by which time the restaurant was deserted. Ginsberg had left a good hour before; he'd been so busy buttering up the elder of the Taft cousins that he'd walked straight past.

'The grown-ups are going to have coffee in the saloon,' Mrs Carter told Hopper. 'I expect you boys will want to go dancing.'

None of us was keen. Hopper had some notion we should find George Dodge and all go down to the cargo hold to look at his father's new motor-car. I said I'd wait for him and Charlie in the foyer; I didn't want to bump into Wallis. As I loitered there Ismay came through on the way to his suite. He said, 'I understand you know Scurra.'

'I've only recently met him.'

'And what do you think of him?'

'Why, I think him … I think he's …' I stopped, unable to think of words sufficiently neutral.

'From that I gather he's made his usual impression.' He stared at me, as if trying to make up his mind. 'I knew him many years ago in France,' he said. 'He's an interesting man … if dangerous.'

'Dangerous!' I said.

'I had reason to ask his advice and he gave it to me.'

'It was bad advice?'

'On the contrary,' he said, 'it was almost certainly good. But I failed to take it.' With that, he wished me goodnight.

Melchett and Hopper had found George in the Veranda Café. He wasn't coming with us but it was all right by him if we wanted a peek at the Lanchester.

'Molly's picked up some bounder who owns a canning factory in Chicago,' explained Hopper. 'George feels he ought to stay and keep an eye on her.'

Melchett was watching me like a hawk but I couldn't help myself. 'I would have thought either Wallis or Ida could do that.'

'Ida would probably hand her over, if asked,' Hopper said. 'And Wallis isn't there.'

We went first to the purser's office and filled out a form authorising our entry into the hold. Hopper had to dash back and get George's signature. Alighting from the elevator on the lower level of G deck we passed along the same route taken by Riley the day before. The heat was tremendous, more so than I remembered, and we walked to the constant vibrating thrum of those hidden, magnificent engines. There was nobody in the cubby hole that served as the baggage office, the man in charge having left his post. We hung on because the kettle on the stove was jiggling to the boil. When at last he did appear he seemed put out at our being there and even had the insolence to suggest we come back in the morning. Hopper put him in his place.

We had to clamber down vertical steps into the hold below. Though a dozen or more switches had been snapped on before our descent, the place was eerily lit, the electric filaments flickering like starlight. We were now below the water-line and the air was filled with ominous creaks and groans and an irregular pinging sound half-way between a tuning fork and the plucking of a violin string. There were two motors, tethered side by side, an ancient Wolseley which Hopper claimed belonged to old Seefax and Dodge's spanking new Lanchester, the latter with its brass headlights, scarlet wheel spokes and dark blue upholstery infinitely superior to the former – at least in Hopper's opinion. My uncle owned a Rolls Royce, as did Jack, but I'd never caught the craze. While Hopper and Charlie fussed round its bonnet discussing horsepower and compression ratios I amused myself inspecting the items nearby. I could see the use for the contents of two tea-chests, one stamped *Hair nets*, the other *Ostrich plumes*, but what was one to make of the several lengths of oak beams bearing the cautionary notice *Not to be mistaken for Ballast*? They were so massive in thickness and so crocheted with worm holes that they must surely have come from a man-of-war or else the roof of a medieval cathedral. Lying athwart them, bound in sacking, teetered a package labelled *Portrait of Garibaldi, Property of C.D. Bernotti*.

Hopper and Charlie had climbed into the Lanchester. Childishly, both began imitating the puttering of an engine and the grinding of gears. Charlie, who was at the wheel, leaned out and squeezed the horn, sending a frog-like honking reverberating round the hold. After a time, mercifully tiring of such foolery, they embarked on one of those fragmentary conversations, to do with women and the future, indulged in by young men late at night. I won't go into what Hopper said about women; some of it was pretty indelicate. God knows what Charlie made of it, his knowledge of such matters extending little further than the pollination of orchids in his father's glass houses. At any rate his contribution was minor, if poignant, mainly that he'd once touched the breast, by mistake, of a very nice girl in Dorset who had first run and told her mother and then vomited.

'You should get yourself rooms of your own in London,' Hopper advised.

'My people would never allow it,' said Melchett.

'There are girls in London,' Hopper boasted, 'who would thank you for caressing them.'

It was different for Hopper, of course. Though only two years older he had an apartment on Fifty-seventh Street and a job in his father's law firm. Being British, Charlie had nothing of his own and nothing to do save ride round the family estate with a gun under his arm, waiting for his father to die. All the same, both insisted they had plans for a golden future which would have little to do with either law or the running of an estate. Quite what it would have to do with wasn't made clear, though Hopper vowed he was going to land the biggest fish that ever flashed in a river.

It's true he was crazy about fishing. When we were boys at Warm Springs he spent whole nights lying on his stomach waiting for the bait to be taken, until his grandmother, catching him fast asleep in the moonlight, a snake a foot away from his face, beat him out of the habit.

I envied them, lolling in that shining automobile, both so sure the future would be different from what had gone before. For myself, I had no such certainties. Jumping into the back of the Wolseley I lay flat and contemplated the heights above and the depths below. Cupping my hands over my ears I imagined it was the ocean that roared in my head. I might have fallen asleep if Hopper hadn't bellowed my name.

'What now?' I called.

'Charlie says you're steamed up over Wallis.'

'Is that so?'

'We all know what she's like, Morgan. The girl has ice in

her veins. I doubt if any man could melt her, not even a husband.'

'I don't wish to discuss it,' I said pompously, and heard his snort of laughter.

It had gone midnight when we climbed up out of the hold. As we returned to the elevator a door opened in the corridor ahead and two men, one in seaman's uniform, stepped out. Between them sagged a third man, knees buckling, head sunk on his breast. A monstrous hissing rolled towards us and ceased as the door clanged shut. I would have passed by had I not recognised Riley. Hopper and Melchett, side-stepping, walked on.

I asked if I could be of assistance. The stricken man was well past middle age, the perspiration plastering his white hair to his scalp. Bare-chested, his sodden trousers smeared with grease and dirt, he looked half drowned. Riley said it was nothing to worry about, simply a matter of heat and exhaustion. Indeed, even as he spoke the old man came to, and, wiping his eyes on the back of one filthy hand made as if to pull back the door.

'He needs rest,' I protested. 'And water.'

After some hesitation on the part of all three, the second man, supporting his comrade round the waist, shambled off along the corridor in the direction of the cargo office. I noticed the sick man had an elaborate crucifixion tattooed on his back, the arms of the Christ spread out across his shoulders.

'They're working double shifts,' said Riley. He began to rub at his soiled uniform with a piece of rag.

'You've coal dust on your cheek,' I said. Taking the rag

from him I offered my handkerchief. Smiling, he took it and dabbed at his face. It wasn't an entirely friendly smile. I was about to wish him goodnight when he said, 'Someone ought to do something about them shifts. They knew the situation before we left Southampton.'

'And what situation was that?' I asked, but before he could reply the two stokers appeared again at the top of the passage.

'Come with me,' he ordered, marching off in the opposite direction, and I followed meekly enough until, reaching a door marked *Crew Only*, he halted and enquired whether I could spare him a few moments. 'I expect,' he said, 'you've better things to do.' Though the words were deferential he made it sound like an accusation.

'Not at all,' I replied, damned if he was going to get the better of me. The room we entered was some sort of night pantry. There was a stove, two chairs, a table with its legs standing in circles of rat poison and a row of shelves stocked with tins of food. On the wall, askew, hung a picture of Captain Smith with his dog.

'I believe you come from Liverpool,' I began, with the notion of putting him at his ease, though indeed he hadn't once addressed me as sir.

'Yes, yes,' he cried impatiently, and motioned me to sit. He himself remained standing, my handkerchief still crumpled in his hand.

'That man,' said he, 'that old geezer you just seen ... he's done a nine hour shift and gone straight into a six-hour one.'

'That seems excessive,' I said.

'It isn't right,' said he. 'It shouldn't be allowed.' In his indignation he kicked at the pellets on the floor. I told him I'd gathered from the steward that the crew was at full muster, to which he replied that was so, but only if circumstances had been normal.

'And aren't they?' I queried.

'Not on your Nellie!' he scoffed. 'What's more, they knew about it before they signed us on. They just didn't bother to hire enough extra men to deal with it.'

'To deal with what?'

'The bloody fire,' he said. 'The bloody fire what's blazing in Number 10 coal bunker.'

I thought of Queen's Island and the hull of the *Titanic* rising up in the drydock of Harland and Wolff. Three million rivets, thrust into coke braziers before being beaten into the overlapping plates, had gone into its construction. She was double-bottomed, the space between big enough for a man to stand up in. Hour upon hour the hammering continued, the clamorous echoes screeching off the tin roofs of the draughtsmen's huts. At the end of the day when the hooter blew and work stopped, the sudden shocking silence plummeted from the leaden skies.

'It's been blazing for days,' said Riley. 'At this rate old man Smith's going to be shamed into asking for the City Fire Department to meet us when we dock.'

I stayed silent, staring at the picture on the wall; it wasn't the same dog I'd fed ginger biscuits. Ginsberg, I thought, had been in the right of it, though quite how the ship had been granted a certificate of sea-worthiness defeated me. I knew about fires from Tuohy. Containment was easy if one kept hosing down the coal; it was the damage done to the so-called steel plates that mattered. They weren't steel at all, just raw iron, and iron weakened under exposure to heat. A picture came into my head of that front room by the harbour, of the hole in the oilcloth, the plaster statue of the Virgin simpering on the mantelpiece. I trembled; it wasn't so much the fire that bothered me, rather the realisation that Tuohy's rantings had been more than fine talk.

'I don't think you should mention this matter further,' I said. 'I'm quite sure the chief engineer is qualified to deal with the situation. And we have the chief designer on board.'

'What do they care?' Riley burst out. 'They won't be doing a fifteen-hour shift in that hell-hole.'

'Neither will you,' I reprimanded, and stood up. Sulkily he opened the door. 'You may keep the handkerchief,' I said, and added, 'I don't expect you to believe it but I've not always lived like this. There was a time when we might have played in the same gutter.' Walking away I was annoyed with myself for being so open with him.

I wasn't ready to go to bed, my thoughts running too wild. Though it was twenty past one by the clock on the landing of the Grand Staircase the lights were still burning in the library. Thomas Andrews was there, alone, scribbling in his notebook, a glass of whisky at his elbow. Remembering our encounter earlier that evening I was all for slipping out again but he spotted me. He immediately brought up the matter of the leaking bath taps and suggested I examine them first thing in the morning and supervise their fixing. When I had done that he wanted me to join him on a thorough inspection of the ship. The experience would be beneficial. It was evident he still thought I was a member of the design team.

He had in mind various adjustments and alterations. The colouring of the private promenade's pebble-dashing was a shade too dark; the appearance of the wicker chairs on the starboard side might be improved if stained green; there were too many screws in stateroom hat hooks; did I think the painting of Plymouth Harbour – here he pointed at a rather dull oil hung above the fireplace – should be replaced with a portrait of a literary figure? Would it not be more suitable for a library?

'It would,' I agreed. I was wondering whether the inspection would include the boiler rooms.

'Shelley,' he said. 'Or perhaps Doctor Johnson.'

'Dickens,' I ventured. 'Then people will know who it is.'

It's possible I had a crush on Andrews. Certainly I admired him. One needs someone to look up to, someone worthy that is, and being fulfilled rather than just rich he was what I judge to be a successful man. He was also a pretty smart dresser and I'd once gone to the lengths of sketching a particular coat he wore – it had a row of tortoise-shell buttons down the front and four on each cuff – and giving it to my tailor to copy. When it was made up I didn't have the nerve to wear it, in case he noticed.

For the rest, he wasn't renowned for his wit, had never said anything to me that stayed in the mind, and one couldn't call him handsome exactly, his face being on the heavy side, though he did have remarkable eyes, blue and candid, and a dimple in his chin. All the same, when I was in his company I quite forgot my plans for the future and if things had been different might have wished for nothing better in this world than to remain in his employ.

He engaged me in a discussion concerning the sirocco ventilating fans in Number 2 engine room. In his opinion they weren't entirely satisfactory.

'I believe you're right, sir,' I said. 'I've just been down on G deck and seen a man carried out with heat stroke.'

'Indeed,' he said, and wrote something in his notebook.

He was good to chat with and learn from, just as long as one kept to the subject of the ship, or rather its design – bring up anything of a more personal nature and he immediately shied off. Stupidly mentioning who I'd dined with that evening I repeated Ismay's remark that heads would roll if we didn't reach full speed.

'Ten o'clock sharp,' he said, cutting me short. 'I suggest we meet outside the gymnasium,' and with that he gathered up his pencil and notebook and made for the door. He walked like a boxer, slightly bow-legged yet light on his feet.

Crushed, I was about to follow at a respectful distance when a tremendous outburst of coughing and spluttering arose from one of the wing armchairs turned to the wall. It was old Seefax, who, thumping the skirting board with his stick, demanded to be turned to the fire. When I'd manhandled his chair into place and prodded the coals into flame, he asked me to ring for a night-cap.

'It's late,' I told him. 'The bar steward has gone off duty.'

'Nonsense,' he wheezed. 'Go and find him,' at which, shouting out to an imaginary attendant, I fetched Andrews' half-filled glass.

'Told you so,' he said. 'They never go off duty, not in a properly run hotel.'

Spilling more than he sipped, he asked, 'What have you been up to? Chasing girls I shouldn't wonder.'

I told him I'd been down to the cargo decks and seen a stoker with a crucifix tattooed upon his back.

'Used to be quite common in the past,' he said. 'They did it hoping to avoid the lash. Same as when they come aboard … you'll see some of the old hands saluting the quarterdeck … the cross used to hang there.'

He then fell into a reverie, eyes fixed on the leaping flames, one parchment claw twisting the black cord from which his spectacles dangled. I waited with him; the ship was as steady as a rock but he was a frail and ancient man and I feared he might fall if left to get to his room on his own.

After some minutes, he said, 'Women are extraordinary creatures. You can never guess what they're capable of.'

I nodded, thinking of Wallis.

'She went out through that window like a chipmunk up a tree. When she clambered back in one could have mistaken her for a nigger woman.'

'Could one,' I said, humouring him.

'It was the smoke from the engine, you see … it was just going through a tunnel.' Then, kicking his feet in delight he cried out, 'That's where I met Scurra.'

His thoughts were dreadfully tangled. The woman had been called Madame Humbert, or perhaps Hubert, and she'd climbed out of a moving train and crawled along its side to reach the next compartment where a wealthy man was having a heart attack–

'Surely not Scurra?' I said.

'No, no, no. That was Crawley ... Crawford ... Cranley .... Having saved his life he left her a fortune. In '97 she spent two thousand dollars on flowers for a party she gave in her house on the Avenue de la Grande Armée.'

'And that's where you met Scurra?'

'I never said that,' he snapped. 'It was in Madrid ... later ... when they arrested her. You'd know about that sort of thing ... noises in the night ... police ... the dock. Always thought her account of the train was fishy ... damned if she could have heard him above the noise of the track.'

I got nothing more out of him on the subject because he was now mumbling about some book on the shelves to do with the battle of Chickamauga in which the Confederates had routed the Union Army. According to him the author had got his facts wrong. 'He should have consulted me,' he muttered, 'I was an eye witness,' though only last Christmas he'd bored Hopper and me rigid with the story of how he'd spent the entire war in Europe, running the blockade single-handed and scuttling cruisers off Cherbourg.

Escorting him from the library I was fortunate enough to find a steward in the foyer who took him off my hands. As I descended the stairs who should I see stepping into the elevator one floor below but Wallis? She was with Ginsberg and I swear he had his hand on her waist.

THREE

Friday, 12th April

Too early the next morning I woke with the fragment of a dream still in my head. It wasn't the one that had disturbed my childhood nights and brought Sissy running. I reckon I'd slept with my arm covering my face because my mouth felt swollen.

I had been walking down a cobbled alleyway between a row of little houses, making for the last one on the left pinned to the arch of a railway bridge. As is the way of dreams I was both in the road and walking up the path – there was a stunted tree, leaves black with soot, standing in a patch of earth near the broken gate. I saw a man on hands and knees, scrabbling at the soil, a piece of newspaper flapping on the sole of his boot. I was carrying a child whose cold, cold cheek was pressed to my own. At that instant a train rattled across the bridge and a belch of black smoke rolled down the street. The man leapt to his feet and with a terrible bellow of rage ran towards me; one moment he was visible, the next the smoke swallowed him up. The scrap of newspaper whirled through the air and masked the child's face. The child turned into myself.

The damnedest thing was, going into the bathroom to shave I noticed my nails were rimmed with dirt. It gave me quite a turn until I remembered that following my trip into the hold I had fallen into bed without washing.

When the steward came in with the coffee pot he remarked I wasn't the only early bird he'd visited that morning. But then, it was fairly usual, he maintained, for passengers to sleep poorly the second night on board. It was a question of getting accustomed to being on water, that and the appearance of the stoker coming up out of the funnel – quite a few people had been upset by that. The two elderly ladies in Stateroom 19 had complained of bad dreams and the middle-aged couple in the Jacobean suite had twice rung for the night steward.

'I slept like a top,' I told him. 'I never dream.'

'Ah, well, sir,' he said, 'That's thanks to youth and an easy conscience.'

It was not yet seven o'clock when I went below to call out the plumbers; I didn't want to run the risk of being late for my appointment with Thomas Andrews. Luckily I was proved right in thinking the fault with the bath taps was nothing more serious than ill-fitting washers, and having selected new ones from the stores and insisted they be put in place right away I was able to go up for my breakfast.

Scurra was seated in the main restaurant with Rosenfelder, the latter in a fever of optimism. Apparently 'Mrs Duff' had told him that Mr Harris, the theatrical producer, was on board. He had only to say the word and she would perform an introduction.

'He's hungry for the limelight,' said Scurra, winking at me.

'There's money in designing dresses for the stage,' Rosenfelder protested. 'Mrs Duff thinks my skills lie in the direction of the flamboyant. There is about me an element of showmanship.'

'You must tell young Morgan what role you have in mind for Adele,' prompted Scurra.

This Rosenfelder did, at some length. It spoilt my breakfast rather, for I had to keep nodding and smiling. If I glanced down to cut my bacon or spread butter on my bread he tapped my knuckles with his teaspoon to ensure attention. He was going to get Adele to sing in the Palm Court that evening; the ship's orchestra would accompany her. This had been Scurra's idea. She would wear the window dress intended for Macy's. That idea had come from Mrs Duff.

'I will then ask Mr Harris to the concert—'

'His very own idea,' interrupted Scurra.

'And in the ticking of a clock myself and the abandoned Adele will make ourselves famous,' concluded Rosenfelder.

I agreed it was a splendid idea and one not likely to fail. Unless, of course, the Fenwicks song-bird didn't choose to sing.

'Pff,' cried Rosenfelder. 'Since when did a woman with two pounds in her purse and no buttons to her coat know such a thing as choice?'

Andrews and his team were at least half an hour late assembling outside the gymnasium. By the time they arrived, Captain Smith, in full dress uniform, medals pinned to his pouting white tunic, the chief engineer, purser, surgeon and chief steward strutting gosling-fashion in his wake, had already begun his daily inspection. It was quite comical the way our two groups kept passing each other,

101

often merging as we went down through the ship examining hand rails and companionways, checking portholes and connecting doors, making notes on the durability of floor coverings, measuring distances between service hatches and tables.

On F deck, forward, something of a kerfuffle ensued when Captain Smith, about to enter the Turkish baths, was confronted by a harridan of a woman stewardess who flew through the doors and barred his way. Apparently he had forgotten that the baths were open to ladies between the hours of ten and twelve each morning.

'You shall not force yourself inside,' she shouted imperiously, taking no heed of the braid on his uniform.

'Madam,' he thundered, 'I have no intention of forcing myself anywhere.'

Discomforted, he turned and blundered into those hard on his heels. Confined in that narrow passage it took time to sort ourselves out and at least two of the design team fell in behind the purser and marched mistakenly off, not to join us again until we reached the Marconi telegraph room. Here I was present, albeit squeezed out into the corridor, when one of the wireless operators read out a message received from the French vessel *La Touraine*, bound from New York to Le Havre, congratulating the *Titanic* on her maiden voyage, wishing her God Speed and warning of ice ahead.

I was half afraid I would encounter Adele during our inspection of the steerage decks. How should I greet her? If I ignored her it was surely on the cards, seeing she roamed over the ship as she pleased, that it would be reported to Scurra, who would then think less of me. In the event, though the public rooms swarmed with men, women and children, mostly emigrants babbling in a mixture of tongues, Adele was not among them.

When we came at last to the engine and boiler rooms, only Smith, Andrews and the chief engineer were allowed access. The rest of us went off to examine the refrigeration area and the cargo holds, through which we tramped to the pinging of that ghostly violin.

Twenty minutes later the engine room detail emerged into the corridor, Andrews mopping his brow, droplets of perspiration sparkling in the Captain's beard. Their glowing faces gave nothing away and neither a reference to fire nor any expression of doubt as to the stability of bulkheads was made in my hearing.

Midday, we rose to the upper levels and gave our attention to the enclosed promenades. Andrews was concerned that a number of steamer chairs had gone from the port side. He instructed me to make a note of it. I hadn't a pencil and turned my back on him, pretending to scribble. Fortunately the missing items were spotted moments later piled behind the door of the Café Parisien. Starboard side, the small grandson of Mrs Brown of Denver was caught finger-drawing on the windows. Told to desist, he put out his tongue. His nurse rubbed the glass clean with her handkerchief and shooed him below.

Once on the boat deck there was a wearisome trudge of its length and an even longer scrutiny of its cranes, winches and ventilators. All were judged to be in good working order. As we passed the base of the forward mast the lookout men of the crow's nest were changing shifts. The two men coming off duty were arguing about a pair of missing night-glasses, one claiming he'd seen them when the ship left Cherbourg, the other adamant he'd not set eyes on them from the day he'd signed on. I heard their exchange quite clearly because our procession had come to a temporary halt while Thomas Andrews greeted Mr and Mrs Carter who were taking a stroll before lunch.

We were further delayed when it came to an inspection of the life-boats, of which there were twenty, including four Englehardt collapsibles, Captain Smith wishing to know if they were sufficiently stocked with emergency blankets. Smiling, the chief steward submitted that they were and had been double checked. All the same, Smith insisted Number 7 boat be lowered immediately so that he could see for himself. Bored with this procedure Andrews strode off before it was completed and led us towards the bows.

I had been waiting impatiently for the moment when we would go up on to the bridge and view the marvels of modern technology within the wheelhouse, and actually had, at last, one foot on the companionway when Andrews, spying a female figure squatting beside a bench midway beneath the first and second funnels, suggested that some-one should go to her assistance. As I had turned to hear what he said and it chanced he was looking straight at me, I was in no position to dodge the request.

The woman was middle-aged and wrapped in furs against the wind. Eccentrically balanced on her haunches, she peered intently at the deck. Upon my enquiring if she had lost anything she pointed at what I took to be a button stuck to the side of the bench bolt. As I bent to pick it up I caught a glint of sliver slime and realised it was a species of mollusc.

'Please don't pull it,' cried the woman. 'It must be detached with the utmost gentleness.'

My efforts weren't altogether successful; there was an audible plop as I prised the thing free.

'What is it?' I asked, thinking she must be some sort of authority on crustacea.

'Possibly a snail?' she questioned, looking at me for affirmation.

We both stood there, gazing down at the object cupped in my hand. I wanted very much to get away and join the others on the bridge. I made as if to tip it into her own hand but she drew back, clutching her furs about her throat.

'Young man,' she said, 'I'm late for luncheon. Be so good as to take the creature indoors and place it in the earth of one of the potted palms.'

I stood at the rail and watched her go, and when the doors swung to behind her tossed the snail overboard. The day was dull, a long smudge of pale light dividing the grey sea from the grey sky. On the horizon a toy boat sat beneath a scribble of smoke. Sprinting back along the deck I was in time to see the design team descending the companionway and moments later our patrol was dismissed.

I went immediately to the smoke-room, found Scurra alone reading a book, and ordered a drink. He observed I looked put out. I told him I'd been all over the ship and having come within yards of the one place that interested me, namely the bridge, had been sent off to deal with a crazy old woman mooning over a snail.

'She ordered me to take it to the lounge,' I said. 'To feed off the palms.'

'But of course you did no such thing. You threw it overboard.'

I was startled, suspecting he'd actually seen the incident.

'And that's not all, is it?' he added. 'Come now, be straight with me. Conversation is useless, don't you think, unless one addresses the truth.'

Though hesitant, at first, scarcely having known until then that the truth was at issue, or indeed in what way I'd been evasive, I soon got the hang of it and poured out more than I intended. This was partly due to his skill in drawing me out and partly because of the heady satisfaction to be gained from talking about oneself. I told him of the fire in the stokehold, my dream of the night before, my involvement with Tuohy in Belfast, my glimpse of Ginsberg with his hand on Wallis's waist. I left out, in connection with the fire, Tuohy's belief that it was legitimate to use sabotage in the struggle for Irish Home Rule, along with his conviction that the ends always justify the means.

Scurra interrupted from time to time, seeking clarity on this or that statement, demanding further details, correcting assumptions. For instance, when I said the Socialist meetings I had attended had shaken my soul and convinced me of the truth of Marx's theory that the real value of commodities lay in the labour embodied in them, he brought me up sharp, insisting that the value of any given product was in direct proportion to demand, and though the theory of surplus value was generally expounded with special reference to capitalistic production, in reality it was independent of the system.

'One must distinguish,' he said, 'between use-value and exchange-value. The air we breathe seldom has exchange-value, but always high use-value, being necessary to life. Philosophically speaking, life may be said to have use-value, but only for the individual. Its exchange is death, which has no value whatsoever unless one is in severe torment.'

'Perhaps,' I said, 'one should substitute worth for value, the latter word leaning too strongly towards the notion of goodness.'

'A point well made,' he said.

At which I glowed with pleasure, though not for long, for he proceeded to tear my new-found beliefs to shreds, not by demolishing the ideas themselves but rather by questioning my own capacity for sound judgement, the young, he asserted, being prey to delusions, awash with misplaced guilt and only too prone, by virtue of unexplained chemical changes and immortal longings, to be struck by the lightning bolt of giddy ideals. He wasn't unkind or dismissive; he eyed me with affection while he laid me bare.

'But I must believe in something,' I heard myself plead, 'some purpose … some cause …'

'Of course you must,' he soothed. 'It's essential at your age. You'll grow out of it as the years pass.'

'But I don't want to grow out of it. There has to be a new way of living … a different way of …'

'Of what, exactly?'

'Of men being equal–'

'But they're not equal,' he said. 'Nor is it desirable that they should be. What would be the value of St Peter's in Rome if every other church in the world was of the same shape and dimensions? What price the flowers in the garden if each were of the same height and colour?'

'I'm talking about people,' I retorted. 'Not flowers.'

'It's entirely to be expected,' he said, 'that a young man such as yourself, rich, pompous, ignorant of the lives of the general mass of humanity, should find himself so persuaded.'

'I haven't met any others,' I protested. 'You wouldn't find Ginsberg or any of the chaps I know worrying about the working man and the worth of his labour.'

'I was talking about you,' he said. 'Your temperament sets you apart. That and your beginnings. Which is why your dream was so explicitly symbolic of darkness and danger.'

I was taken aback that he should be so blunt. Though I supposed some of my uncle's generation were acquainted with the facts of my early life, none had come out with it so plain. It's true that old Seefax had crossed the line the evening before, but then he could be excused on the grounds of near senility.

'Last night,' I said, anxious to change the subject, 'Mr Seefax told me a confused story about a woman crawling along the outside of a train. You know how he rambles. He said it was in Madrid, where he met you.'

'So it was ... at a reception given by the Ambassador. Seefax was negotiating with some arms manufacturer and I was attending the trial of Madame Humbert. An extraordinary case, don't you think?'

'I didn't understand it,' I confessed.

'She made up a pack of lies about saving the life of a wealthy American who was having a heart attack in the next carriage. Hearing his groans and finding the door to his compartment locked, she claimed to have climbed out of the window and gone to his aid. Later, she produced letters purporting to have come from him, promising he would leave her his fortune. All forged, of course. There never was an American, rich or otherwise. On the strength of these letters she lived the life of Madame Pompadour until found out. An ingenious woman, don't you agree?'

'Very,' I said. 'If shameful.'

'Except in degree, no more shameful than your own action of earlier this morning.'

'What action was that?' I demanded, shocked.

'Pretending to come to the aid of an elderly woman and consigning a snail to the depths,' he said, smiling gleefully. 'Both acts are the product of thoughtlessness and from the snail's point of view yours is the more reprehensible.'

We both laughed, he so much so that he had to blot his eyes with a none too clean handkerchief. Recovering, he asked why I didn't declare myself to Wallis. 'At your age,' he said, 'you have nothing to lose. She can either respond favourably or let you down gently. Very few women are deliberately cruel. It's not in their natures. Besides, all women thrive on admiration.'

I said I wouldn't know what words to use. Wallis was

such an unapproachable girl, so downright pure and straight.

'Good heavens,' he murmured. 'How extraordinarily little you know about women, and that one in particular.'

We didn't lunch together; he said he wasn't hungry and preferred to nap until tea-time. It wasn't until he'd gone that I realised he'd told me nothing about himself.

*

At lunch, Hopper fell out with Ginsberg. It was quite a spat and became so heated that Guggenheim sent Kitty Webb over to tell them to lower their voices. I wasn't present myself and only heard of it second-hand from Hopper when I ran into him and Melchett on my way to the library later that afternoon. Hopper admitted that at one point it had nearly come to blows. Of course, they'd all drunk a fair amount. Molly Dodge had burst into tears.

'Molly?' I said incredulously.

'Ginsberg was raving on about the German navy again,' Melchett explained. 'That and the fiendish nature of the German character. He's an awful bully when he gets on his hobby horse. He said the Kaiser was a madman and out to ruin us all.'

'Why the devil should Molly care what Ginsberg thinks of the Kaiser?' I asked, bewildered.

'On account of her mother being German,' said Hopper. 'A fact Ginsberg kept dinning into her. He held all Germans were crazy, her mother in particular ... she shot herself, if you remember ... I tried to quieten him ... Molly was trembling … but he called me a bloody fool and said I was too damned blind to see which way the wind was blowing.'

'She never knew her mother,' I said.

'I jumped up, suggested we go outside to sort the matter out, and Kitty Webb came over to see what was up.'

'Ginsberg backed off,' said Melchett, 'because of Guggenheim. The man's a frightful crawler.'

'The mother killed herself,' I said, 'when Molly was two months old.'

'One's mother is always sacred,' Melchett said primly. 'Whether one knew her or not.' It wasn't a remark I could argue with.

In the hope of finding inspiration in some poetry book, I was all set on going to the library to write a letter to Wallis. Needless to say, I didn't breathe a word of my intentions to either Melchett or Hopper. They were off down to G deck for a knockabout on the racquets court and pestered me to join them. At first I argued, protesting I had more important things to do, and then gave in, fearing they might harass me to the point where I gave myself away.

The steward was in my stateroom when I went there to change, unlocking the porthole. He said he'd be back in an hour to close it, once the fresh air had circulated. He was flushed in the face and none too steady on his feet, but I let it go. His was a servile enough position and I reckoned he needed a prop to sustain him.

It wasn't an evenly matched game. F. White was on duty on court and made up a pair with Melchett. The two of them were streets ahead of Hopper and me, White being a professional and Melchett having excelled at the game during his

111

years at Eton. He had a powerful backhand and a beautiful turn of wrist. When he flung up the ball and lent his head back to serve, his teeth gleamed under the lights. Though he should have known better, White kept calling out, 'Excellent stroke, sir,' and smirking.

Hopper was too tiddly to hit the ball straight on; his shots went all over the place. As a second string he was a liability and in the middle of the fourth game, our opponents well on the way to winning a love rubber, I lunged forward and felt a stinging blow to my head, either from his racquet or the belt of his trousers, and staggered about the court, blood streaming from a cut above the eye. It wasn't serious and we hadn't had a hope of winning, but I groaned a bit to let Hopper stew. I have never been foolish enough to believe it's the game that counts.

Not that I could keep it up for long, not with Hopper carrying on in such a remorseful manner. I swear I saw tears in his eyes as he dabbed at my forehead with the sleeve of his pullover. 'What a fool I am,' he kept repeating, 'what an absolute fool.'

'I don't suppose you've got any sticklebacks with you?' I asked, but he was too upset to catch the reference and looked more concerned than ever, convinced I was delirious. Once, long ago, he'd pitched me from the orchard wall and sent me spread-eagled on to the melon patch, my cheek splitting open on the shard of a broken pot. Thinking he'd killed me he'd run and hidden down by the boat-house, until, after nightfall, I was dispatched to look for him. 'Are you alive?' he'd demanded, seeing me standing in moonlight. Then, as if to reassure himself of the truth, he'd stretched out his hand to take the warmth of my face on his fingertips, spat into the grass and swaggered off ahead to the house. Before I went to sleep he gave me his jar of sticklebacks. In the morning he took them back again.

White was all for treating me like a big soft girl, expecting me to lie down, but I said I had to meet someone urgently. Hopper, never one to stay contrite for long, having first insisted he accompany me to the lift suddenly remembered he wanted to send a wireless message to a woman he knew in Boston and abruptly left me. I shook off Melchett by telling him I needed to be quiet.

Armed with two volumes of poetry and a copy of Shakespeare's *Romeo and Juliet* I sat down at a library table and struggled to write to Wallis. I soon gave up on Shakespeare, having forgotten that Romeo's intentions were honourable and how often Juliet blushed. Besides, considering it was life I was after, the emphasis on death was unsuitable. Nor were the poems of much help, the only lines that appealed, *When we are gone, love, Gone with the breeze, Woods will be sweet, love, Even as these*, striking me as more expressive of an affair drawing to a close rather than one just starting. In the end, after much crossing out I simply wrote, *Dear Wallis, I think you're wonderful. Please, I must talk to you. Will you meet me tonight at seven o'clock on the port side promenade?* I had wanted to suggest we meet on deck but I knew what a flap girls got into when they thought their hair might be blown about. I had just put my name to this admittedly gauche note when a small drop of blood from the cut above my eye fell on to the page; it landed exactly beside my signature and became star-shaped. Far from looking messy, I reckoned it

113

lent emotional significance. Just then Rosenfelder sat down opposite me.

'She won't do it,' he wailed. 'She absolutely refuses.' His cheeks wobbled in distress.

'You mean Adele won't sing?' I said.

'She will sing her head off ... but not in my dress. Where is Scurra?'

'Why won't she wear it?'

'She says it is not suitable for her song. She has in mind something oriental. I need Scurra.'

I said I believed Scurra was resting but would be in the Palm Court at tea-time. Pointing at my forehead he asked if I had been fighting. He had heard of a fracas in the dining room. One or two of the older passengers had complained of the younger members not being able to hold their drink.

'It was Ginsberg,' I told him. 'Ginsberg and Hopper arguing about the Kaiser.'

'Such things the young bother themselves with,' he marvelled, looking heavenwards and clapping his hands like a child at a party.

I didn't immediately slip the letter under Wallis's door, believing it more prudent to turn the words over in my mind while taking a stroll on deck. There were several couples at the rail, admiring the dramatic aspect of the sky. The afternoon was dying, the horizon piled with black clouds tipped with silver light. Even as I watched the blocked sun burst forth, dazzlingly pale and ringed with crimson as it sank towards the sea. A little ratty dog skidded towards the rail and jumped upwards, jaws wide, thinking he might catch it. This so perfectly mirrored my own deluded behaviour that I took out my letter and was in the act of casting it overboard when a sudden gust of wind tore it from my hand and blew it back on deck, at which the dog, cheated of the sun, pounced on it and trotted triumphantly away. Horrified that others might read what I'd so foolishly written, I gave chase.

I was led the devil of a dance along the full length of the deck, and just when I thought I had the wretched animal cornered it leapt the iron gate separating the first and second class areas and disappeared from sight.

Convinced that at any moment the thief would deposit my letter at the feet of its owner and not wanting to be identified, I turned hurriedly back. No sooner had I reached the gymnasium doors when something amazing happened – the dog appeared round the corner of the port promenade and racing towards me dropped my letter on deck. Miraculously, though the paper was a little damp at the centre and the speck of blood slightly fuzzy, my love-note was otherwise unspoilt. I was so elated by this stroke of good fortune that I decided to go at once to Wallis's room.

I was advancing cautiously along the starboard corridor of A deck – I didn't want to encounter either Wallis, Ida or Molly – when who should approach from the opposite end but Scurra. We met in the middle and expressed surprise at seeing one another. I said I'd taken a wrong turning and he agreed that it was easy to get lost in a ship of this size. We retraced our steps and entered the lift, he remarking that he'd slept for two hours.

'I had a knockabout on the racquets court,' I told him.

'So I see,' he said, looking at my forehead. 'One should

never dive for the ball. The trick is to let the ball come to you, don't you think?'

He then told me he'd been thinking over our conversation of earlier that day and come to the conclusion that he'd been too hard on me. After all, ideals were important and it was good to have the courage of one's convictions.

'I'm delighted you think that,' I said, to which he replied that convictions were worthless unless based on insight.

We both got out of the lift on C deck and I assumed he was going to his quarters. We were nearing the door of my stateroom when he took a tumble. The corridor was narrow and we were walking side by side, jostling one another, and suddenly he tripped and fell down. He sprang up again immediately but the blood had drained from his face. I was about to commiserate and give him my arm when I realised such an action would considerably embarrass him. Reasoning that he was a proud man and one not capable of accepting help, I walked on, opened my door and asked him casually enough if he'd care to come in for a drink.

The room was cold; McKinlay had forgotten to close the porthole. I was tugging it shut when I heard Scurra exclaim, 'Good God.' I turned, thinking he had taken ill, but he was standing in front of my mother's picture.

'The painting,' he said. 'How strange to see it here on this particular wall. Surely it can't be part of the ship's furnishings?'

'It isn't,' I said. 'It was in my cousin's house and I'm taking it home to my uncle.'

'Do you know who the subject is?'

'I do,' I replied, and fetched whisky and glasses from the

cabinet. He sat down on the sofa and regarded me steadily while I poured out our drinks. I was shaking. I knew instinctively that he was about to tell me something, something I'd been waiting to be told since first setting eyes on him in the breakfast room of the South Western Hotel. I saw him more clearly than I had before, noticed his large hands, his muscular neck, the threads of grey in his dark hair. For once, his eyes were sober, watchful. When I gave him his glass his fingers touched mine and I snatched my hand away, not wanting him to feel I was trembling.

At last, he said, 'Don't misunderstand me. I didn't know her well. I can tell you very little on that score.'

'Where was it?' I asked.

'In Provence. Twenty-four years ago.' He explained that he'd been in Paris on business and had cause to go south, to Aix, to stay in the country house of a dealer in pictures. One day they had gone to the studio of a painter called Cézanne where the dealer had bought a still life and two portraits, one of an old man, the other of a girl–

'My mother,' I said.

'I knew her name and knowing of the connection advised the dealer to get in touch with your uncle. He dislikes modern works, as you know, but in this instance I thought he would make an exception.'

'And did you meet my mother?'

'On two occasions only. Once in the painter's studio and once in the local café.'

'What was she like?'

'She was just a girl. A little like the painting, a little like you.'

117

'I look like her?'

'A very slight resemblance … something about the eyes. It's a long time ago. If I had known I would be interrogated I might have taken more notice.'

'I thought you did know,' I said, startling myself.

'My dear boy,' he remarked dryly. 'Even I can't be expected to know everything.'

'You've told me very little,' I cried, and was surprised at how angry I sounded. 'I need to know more.'

'There's little more to tell,' he protested. 'A girl sitting on a lop-sided stool, a smell of rabbit glue from the iron pot on the stove, a smudge of cobalt blue on the stone flags of the floor–'

'Who was she with?'

'The first time she was alone, save for Cézanne. The second, she was waiting on tables.'

For some moments I couldn't speak.

'I've upset you,' he said. 'Forgive me, but you asked to be told.'

'It's hard,' I said, my voice wobbling, 'to think of her serving in a café.'

'Come now,' Scurra chided. 'I thought you believed in the dignity of labour and the equality of man.'

'I do,' I shouted.

'But not when it approaches too close to home, is that it?'

He was wrong. My thoughts were not really of my mother at all. In the newspaper cuttings she had figured as a widow whose husband, unnamed, had died abroad. I had never thought of my father, never heard him described, never known anyone who had spoken with him, not even my uncle. My mother and he had met in London, she had eloped to Paris with him, they had begotten me and two months before I was born he had vanished from the picture. It was my mother who came into my dreams and that only as someone I cried out for when the old woman made those terrible noises and the yellow bile jerked on to my cheek.

'And did you never meet *him*?' I blurted out.

'Who?' Scurra asked. He was sitting on the edge of the sofa, shoulders hunched, his expression guarded.

'My father.'

'She was alone,' he said, evading the question.

'Is it possible he's still alive?'

And then he understood me, and hope died, for he said, 'I'm not your father, Morgan.'

Of course I pretended he'd misunderstood me, that I hadn't thought any such thing, and of course he said he knew I hadn't and even if I had that he would have taken it as a compliment. After that we both laughed, fell silent, and then I wept.

Scurra got to his feet, cleared his throat several times, took out his handkerchief and thrust it at me. He walked up and down while I remained standing in the middle of the room, shoulders heaving, the tears running down my cheeks. He didn't tell me to be quiet or urge me to pull myself together. Now and then he squeezed my shoulder as he passed.

I suspect my loss of control had much to do with the blow to my forehead. Delayed shock, I shouldn't wonder. The odd thing was, I didn't feel in the least ashamed, though thinking about it now it was a pretty unmanly way to

119

behave, and had it been the other way round and it was Scurra who broke, or any other fellow for that matter, I'd have wished the ground to swallow me.

Gradually, I grew calmer and Scurra barked, 'Blow your nose.' Then he ordered me to go and bathe my face, and when I'd done so and emerged restored, he refilled my glass, waved my apologies aside and told me to sit down.

'When you first saw me,' he said, 'you thought you had known me before. Am I correct?'

'Something like that,' I replied.

'We have met twice before,' he said. 'The second time was ten years ago in Luxor, when I was staying at the Winter Palace and joined your uncle's party at a picnic amid the ruins of Karnak–'

'I don't remember,' I cried.

'You had climbed on to the feet of Rameses II and were throwing hard-boiled eggs at your friend Van Hopper.'

'I don't remember,' I repeated.

'Nor do I expect you to remember the first time,' he said. 'You were five years old and sitting in the office of the superintendent of an orphanage in Manchester.'

I was so agitated, so astounded that he had known me before I had known myself, that I jumped up and would have seized him by the shoulders if he hadn't pushed me away and warned that if I didn't compose myself and remain seated he wouldn't utter another word. I did as I was told; there was something of the lion tamer about him as he strode back and forth, stabbing the air with one finger as his clawed mouth spat out the facts.

'I was instructed by your uncle's lawyers to make enquir-

120

ies into your background. You had the right name and nothing else. You had been brought to the orphanage by a man called Mellor, landlord of the house you had previously lived in with your mother. The two rooms on the back of the ground floor were occupied by a wealthy spinster named Barrow who had £1,600 invested in India stock and a considerable sum in an account with the Salford and Manchester City Savings Bank. She also owned the leaseholds of both a public house and a barber's shop. Under her bed she kept a tin trunk containing never less than £400 in gold. It was evident she had no need to live in such squalid surroundings, but it was thought she'd become addicted to alcohol and been obliged to leave various other premises on account of it. Miss Barrow had taken a particular fancy to you and when your mother died of influenza, one week after your third birthday, she took you in, neither the landlord nor the authorities raising any objection.'

Here, Scurra paused, presumably to see if I was about to raise an objection of my own, but I held my tongue. Most of what he had told me, save for Miss Barrow being the proprietor of a public house, I already knew of from Jack's newspaper cuttings.

'In summertime, eighteen months later, Miss Barrow became ill with stomach pains and took to her bed. Her upset was first put down to a piece of fish that had gone off and then to the unwholesome gases rising from the river below her window. In September, having been seen by two doctors on four occasions, she grew worse. During her last days she suffered from continuous vomiting and diarrhoea, her

121

one comfort derived from the closeness of the child she insisted on keeping beside her in the bed.'

He paused again, but I looked at him steadily enough. By the matter of fact way in which he catalogued such dreadful details I was more than ever convinced he must be a lawyer.

'Two months later the landlord and his wife were arraigned on a charge of murder and Mellor found guilty of putting arsenic, obtained from the soaking of fly-papers, into the Valentine's meat-juice his wife had so assiduously spooned into their lodger. He was hanged at Pentonville. As your name had featured in the trial, though only in one sentence in one London newspaper, enquiries were set in motion to find you.'

I gathered he had finished, for he looked at me expectantly. Noticing my shoe lace was undone, I bent to tie it.

'A fortunate turn of events,' he said. 'Don't you agree?'

I uttered not a word. He urged me to take a sip of the whisky but I shook my head; my thoughts were jumbled enough. Now that he had spewed out all he knew he appeared irritated by my silence. He yawned, took out his watch and expressed surprise at the time. 'I'll leave you now,' he said, 'perhaps we shall meet at dinner,' and strode to the door. Opening it, he hesitated, then turned to look at me. He said, 'We are like lambs in the field, cropping the grass under the eye of the butcher who chooses first one then another to meet his requirements. On our good days we have no thought for the tribulations fate may have in store for us – sickness, mutilation, loss of reason, death –'

'What did I look like when I was five years old?' I interrupted. 'Was I small for my age?'

122

'Average. Your head was shaved to discourage lice.'

'What did I say? Did I mention my mother?'

'You asked after Miss Barrow and a toy horse she had given you.'

'I have no recollection of the horse,' I said, but the door was already closing behind him.

*

Some men shy away from society when life deals an underhand blow. That's not my way; I need people to restore my spirits and could scarcely wait to join the others for dinner. In Scurra's company it was necessary to contemplate the exquisite darkness of the world, and though not melancholy by nature I had been touched by shadows. It wasn't that he'd been overly brutal in his summary of my past – he had, after all, omitted to mention that my mother mouldered in a public grave – rather that he'd been less than sensitive in regard to my infant self. It wouldn't have cost him much to invent a gleam of intelligence in the baby-blue eyes beneath the shaven scalp.

I was in my dressing-gown preparing to bathe when the steward knocked at the door. In my haste to get rid of him I was foolishly quick in pardoning him for not securing the porthole earlier. He took advantage and loitered over his task. Glancing at me curiously he remarked that an infusion of cold tea was very good for swellings. I jumped to the conclusion that my eyes were puffy and spun him a yarn about an unaccompanied dog having run off with my newspaper. 'I ran the full length of the ship in pursuit,' I said. 'The wind made my eyes water.'

'Possibly the dog was a retriever, sir,' he replied. Taking my evening clothes from the wardrobe he laid them out on the bed. 'Certain winds,' he continued, 'are considered to have a detrimental effect on both man and beast. Under their influence the most peaceful of men have been known to lose control and act in an uncharacteristically energetic way. It happened to me once on the Mediterranean run. By inclination I'm what one might call timid, yet come the mistral I set about the ship's doctor with a poker and laid him out cold, and all because I took a sudden dislike to the way he sprinkled sugar on his pudding.' Here, he was about to empty the pockets of my day coat when I remembered the note to Wallis and shouted out for him to leave things alone, at which he pursed his lips, put the whisky tumblers on to a tray and flounced from the room.

I realised what he'd been raving about when I caught sight of myself in the glass. Obviously Hopper had told no one of the outcome of the racquets game and all and sundry of the scrap in the dining room. Emptying the pockets of my tweed coat and transferring the contents to my evening jacket, I rang the bell repeatedly. When at last McKinlay arrived I apologised for my brusqueness, handed him a dollar bill and asked to be brought a jug of cold tea. He thanked me and took his time in returning.

I spent a good half-hour bathing my forehead, with disappointing results. It was just as well I'd been prevented from delivering my letter to Wallis; my brow had begun to bulge and the skin circling my eye was unmistakably foxed with purple. Just as I was thinking the worst of McKinlay, imagining he'd deliberately mixed too little tea with too much water, he came in and gave me a black satin eye-patch to wear. The effect was pretty dashing.

I arrived in the foyer in time to hear the bugle blow for the serving of dinner and was at once a focus of interest, not all of it friendly. My piratical appearance was taken as proof positive of my part in the fracas over the mental stability of Kaiser Wilhelm and Molly Dodge's mother. Kitty Webb took my side. When Guggenheim swept past with an ill-concealed glance of disapproval, I heard her say, 'Benny, it wasn't Morgan. Sweet Jesus, he wasn't even there.'

Lady Duff Gordon thought she was behaving like a brick in going out of her way to greet me. 'Morgan,' she cried loudly, 'now the evening can begin.' When I held her gloved hand in mine she whispered, 'Boys will be boys, but this particular boy must be more careful than most of causing offence.' There wasn't time to ask her why.

Wallis and Ida Ellery were seated at Melchett's table. The band was playing something from *The Chocolate Soldier* as I approached. My heart beat like a drum when Wallis looked up and smiled. I felt she could read me like a book and was thankful for the circle of black satin attached to my face; one eye at least would remain a blank page.

I had sat down and was still rehearsing what I might say to her when Rosenfelder, followed by Ginsberg, rushed into the restaurant. The tailor was looking very dapper, hair sleeked back behind his ears, a jewelled pin stuck in his shirt front. 'Scurra has struck a bargain,' he called out as he bustled further down the room to join the Duff Gordons' table. From this distance he continued to communicate with me by means of sign language, hands clasped in prayer, mouth open like a Swiss yodeller. I took it he meant that Adele was going to wear his dress when she sang.

When I turned back from him I was staggered to find Ginsberg seated opposite. Melchett looked uncomfortable but neither of the girls seemed put out. Far from appearing chastened, Ginsberg was as cocky as ever and proceeded to monopolise the conversation. He maintained I was lucky not to have lost my sight and that Hopper should be shot for going on to the racquets court half sober. 'No wonder he's lying low,' he said, which was rich coming from him.

Wallis was affable towards me and even went to the lengths of pressing my foot with hers, though that was when Ginsberg said something asinine about one of the Taft cousins and knocked a glass over. Not that she was really listening. Much of the time she either gazed round the room or stared at the door. If Ginsberg hadn't been so boring I might have thought she was waiting for someone. When he asked if she was prepared to bet on our time of arrival in New York – he'd been down to the purser's office and learnt we'd covered 386 miles since yesterday lunch-time – she turned on him. 'Not all of us are so eager for the voyage to end,' she snapped.

She looked awesomely beautiful, eyes like brown velvet, cheeks tinted rose, a little blue vein palpitating in the hollow of her throat. In my head I pretended I'd delivered the note and that she and I had met on the promenade and come to an understanding. When dinner was over she would first allow me to take her into my arms on the dance floor and after that – but here, such a picture flashed into my mind of what would happen in the *after* that I was seized with a fit of trembling so intense that the spoon in my hand clattered against the sides of my pudding dish. Only Ida noticed, and being kind, feigned she hadn't.

'You'll be interested to know,' Ginsberg said, addressing me, 'that Scurra holds equally fierce views on the beastly properties of anything German.'

Melchett groaned.

'And he speaks from experience. His lip was damaged from the recoil of a Mauser rifle.'

'He was bitten by a parrot,' I said. I was distracted by the sight of Rosenfelder mounting the orchestra rostrum. He spoke to the violinist who nodded then shooed him away with his bow.

'You're both mistaken,' Wallis said. 'I happen to know Scurra was gored by a bull in Cadiz.'

At which moment the band finished their piece and a hubbub of shushing arose from the Duff Gordons' table, whereupon Rosenfelder, climbing on to a chair, called for silence. He was only partially successful, in that Mrs Brown of Denver had evidently just delivered the punch line to one of her risqué stories; a bellow of laughter from the gentlemen at her table obliterated his opening words.

'... in half an hour in the Palm Court,' he concluded, stabbing his cigar in that direction, and beaming clambered from view.

'What's Rosenfelder blabbing about now?' asked Ginsberg.

'He's organised a recital,' said Wallis. 'A lady called Miss Baines is to sing for us.'

I was surprised she was so well informed and wondered if she knew that the 'lady' in question was travelling steerage. Not wishing to ask her outright, I observed instead that it was strange we hadn't known of Miss Baines' existence before now. Wallis gave one of her enigmatic smiles and said that most things were strange, and none more so than men.

When she and Ida went off to the powder room, Melchett, spotting Molly Dodge at the Carters' table, declared he was going over to enquire whether she was feeling better. 'She was terribly upset earlier on,' he said, and added for Ginsberg's benefit, 'Which is hardly surprising, is it?' Ginsberg didn't bat an eyelid. At Melchett's departure he moved chairs and sat beside me. In spite of putting his mouth to my ear he spoke in such a low voice that I had to strain to hear him. 'Good news,' he whispered. 'I've heard on the grape-vine that the fire's almost out.'

I hesitated, then asked, 'Do they know what caused it?'

'Insufficient hosing down of the coal,' he said. 'I guess they were in a hurry on account of meeting the departure date.'

I'd never really looked at him properly, certainly not at such close quarters, and was astonished at how pale his skin was and how crimson his mouth in comparison. He drew back slightly and studied me in return. 'You don't seem convinced,' he said.

Of course I shrugged him off and made light of the whole thing, but I'm not sure he was fooled. My feelings towards

128

him were thoroughly ambivalent; on the one hand I detested him and on the other – well, I already knew he was pretty confident, which is not to be scoffed at. That day beside the Thames, when he'd thrown himself down on the grass after I'd challenged him to a fight, he'd shouted, 'What on earth will it prove if I knock you out?' It was his assumption that I'd be the loser, rather than the other way round, that had got through to me. It was damnably irritating, of course, but still impressive. I began to wonder whether I shunned him because everybody else did, and for the same reasons; we instantly detect in others those faults most common to ourselves.

A large crowd gathered in the Palm Court after dinner. Lady Duff Gordon saw to that, rounding us up like so many sheep. Nor were we allowed to sit where we pleased, the tables having been removed and the chairs rearranged in front of the flight of stairs leading up to the mirrored doors of the à la carte restaurant. To the right of the stairs stood a three-pronged candle stand, five foot in height, topped with virgin candles. The orchestra sat below the stairs and to the left.

I must say Lady Duff Gordon was right in thinking Rosenfelder had a touch of the showman. He didn't call for silence but simply stood there, arms outstretched, as if gathering in the voices. When it was almost quiet he mounted the steps, lit the candles, turned, signalled to a steward who waited by the doors into the foyer, and the next moment the electric lights went out. There was an immediate hush. Lit thus, magical with leaping shadows, the stair landing took on the aspect of a stage. Bowing, Rosenfelder announced he

129

had the honour to present, straight from the Opera House in Paris, Miss Adele Baines. Dramatically he strode left, to the swing doors opening on to the enclosed promenade, and pushed them wide. A blast of night air tore at the candles and sent the flames rippling. The buzz of conversation started up again, though not so loudly as before. A dog, similar to the one who had pounced upon my letter, turned round and round on the Axminster carpet and subsided, muzzle on paws. Several women could be heard complaining of the cold. A figure appeared in the doorway and suddenly there was no sound at all save for a unified intake of breath.

She was dressed in Japanese costume and wore a black wig above the chalk-white mask of her face. Tippy-toeing, as though her feet were bound, she advanced to the centre of the landing. She appeared sightless, for the eyes beneath the painted lids were so pale in colour as to be invisible, and there she waited, divinely tall, her two hands pressed to the silken breast of her poppy-red kimono. Then the orchestra began to play.

I'd seen productions of *Madame Butterfly* on many occasions in London, Madrid, and New York, and always found the story unconvincing and sentimental. Who can believe that a woman, and a Japanese one at that, is capable of such passion? I'd certainly not expected to be disturbed by Adele's interpretation of Cio-Cio-San. I had regarded her behaviour of the day before, when she had run towards the rail, as nothing more than a calculated piece of play-acting performed for the benefit of Scurra, but now, as she sang in candlelight, I saw it differently. It wasn't just her voice that moved me, though that was pure and thrilling enough in tone, nor the contrast between the chill and doleful mask of her face and the burning intensity she brought to the hackneyed words, but rather the realisation that she had indeed been prepared to die of love.

Un-bel dí, ve-dre-mo, le var-si un fil di fu-mo …
Sul l'estremo confin del mare
Poi la nave appare
Vedi? E venuto …

Here, she looked towards the swing doors, one hand clutched to her heart, the other pitched against the air as if pressing back a joy that threatened to overwhelm her. An astonishing thing happened; we too turned to glance in that direction, and in spite of the darkness it was possible to believe she glimpsed that dazzling uniform against the deep blue sky …

I do not run to greet him. Not I!
I rest upon the rise of the hillside
and there wait …

Now she was faltering a little, caught betwixt ecstasy and despair–

Wait for a long time, never tiring
of the long waiting …

And I did know then, suddenly and dreadfully, how cruelly she had been kept waiting, for hope springs eternal, as they say, even though the one who waits, be it a woman on a hillside or a child swinging its legs on an orphanage bench, already divines that the mandate of heaven is lost and the waiting must last for ever.

When Butterfly had finished – *He will call, he will call, my little orange blossom … tiente la tua paura, io son sicura fede l'aspetto* – and we'd clapped our hardest and roared for more – Adele declined – the electric lights came on and the tables were put back in place. Almost at once, what we had felt faded and nothing remained of the experience save for three wisps of smoke spiralling from the blown-out candles. The orchestra struck up a turkey-trot and Molly Dodge inveigled Melchett on to the dance floor.

I went to sit with Lady Duff Gordon and her party, where we were presently joined by a triumphant Rosenfelder and Adele, the latter still in costume. On my murmuring to Rosenfelder that it was a pity his dress hadn't been shown he assured me it would be worn on Sunday night at dinner. 'Scurra has fixed it,' he whispered. 'I am a made man. She is now the cynosure of all eyes and will receive the attention due to an Empress.'

Adele was perfectly at ease in our company, sipping champagne and dabbing at the corners of her plum-coloured lips with a scarlet sleeve peppered with moth-holes. She said she had been disconcerted at first by the brisk tempo set by the violinist. When she had last sung the aria – it was at a concert given by the staff of Fenwicks – it had gone slower. She had also held a fan which had been used to some effect to signify the motion of the waves fluttering towards the harbour. We agreed this was a masterly touch and tut-tutted our regret at having missed it.

Lady Duff Gordon asked whether she would be appearing at a concert hall in New York. If she was it would be simplicity itself to arrange a supper party afterwards.

'That would be kind,' Adele said, 'but I have decided to retire from the stage. My voice is not in any way remarkable.'

'But you have such presence,' cried Lady Duff Gordon, 'such charisma. I don't think I've ever seen Cio-Cio-San portrayed better, and I include the great Madame Krusceniski.' She was so anxious to convey the sincerity of her praise that she leaned across and seized Adele by the wrist. 'My dear,' she insisted, 'you have a stroke of genius.'

'I don't wish to sing any more,' Adele said. 'I no longer feel the finger stroke of love.'

I was puzzling over this pretentious phrase when Rosenfelder demanded matches for his cigar; he had used up his own in lighting the candles. Digging into my pocket I spilled the contents on to the table. The snapshot thrust upon me in Manchester Square fell face down beside the keys to Princes Gate. On the back was written in pencil, *To G.R. from A.B, 1909*. Rosenfelder was reaching out for the matches – I caught the glint of his signet ring – when Adele roughly pushed his hand away. Stabbing at the square of card with her finger, she asked, 'How did you come by this?' Her colourless eyes, outlined in black, stared into my soul.

'It's a curious story,' I replied, somewhat startled, and told it, after which Adele picked up the snapshot, stood, swayed, clutched at the table, dislodging a glass in the process, and drifted backwards to the floor.

Scurra appeared out of nowhere and knelt at her side. He touched her neck with the back of his hand and felt the pulse in her wrist. That wretched dog trotted over to see what was up and he kicked it away like a man getting rid of mud on his shoe.

Adele recovered quickly. She apologised for alarming Lady Duff Gordon and was led away by Scurra who seated her in a far corner of the room and fanned her with a napkin. Lady Duff Gordon told everyone within hearing that Adele was a sensitive artiste. Her husband frowned and seemed offended by the whole business, but then, it was his glass Adele had knocked over. Rosenfelder was mystified. 'I thought it was you who would faint,' he told me. 'Your face was as white as hers. What was on the photograph? Who is this man who died on the pavement?'

I might have enlightened him if Scurra hadn't beckoned. Adele was smiling. As I sat down beside her she cried out, 'Thank you, thank you, my dear friend;' seizing my hand she kissed it. She begged to hear the whole story again, and interrupted constantly. What had happened to his coat? Had the police removed it from the railings? Did he utter her name? Had he suffered? Heart attacks were painful, were they not? To this last question Scurra answered that strokes were worse. A cardiac arrest such as her lover appeared to have had would cause no more than a few seconds of discomfort. She asked me what the children had been singing.

'What children?'

'The ones going into the park over the road.'

'I don't think they were singing,' I faltered. 'It was just the way their voices sounded at a distance.'

'Like bells,' she remarked. 'Like tinkling bells.' She thanked me once more and said she was tired and would like to talk further in the morning. Scurra offered to accompany her below decks but she refused; it was easy to bypass the barriers if one took the Captain's route. Giving a perfectly radiant smile, she left.

'I don't understand why she's so cheerful,' I burst out. 'I expected her to leap for the ocean again. Is it possible she didn't love him after all?'

'You don't understand women,' he said, which was true enough. 'Given the choice, desertion or bereavement, a woman will pick the latter every time. A sensible enough preference, don't you agree? At least she knows where he is.'

And then, of course, his shoulders heaved with laughter, in which I joined because I couldn't help myself. I guess it was his way of puncturing false concern. It's bunkum to suppose we can be touched by tragedies other than our own.

I suggested a stroll together on deck before bed. He hesitated and then agreed. As we rose from the table Wallis approached. She wanted to know if Miss Baines had recovered from her fainting fit. Scurra answered that she had.

'We're just going out to take the air,' he said. 'I shouldn't think we'll be long.'

'What is the time?' she asked, and without consulting his watch Scurra told her it was ten forty-five, which was incor-

135

rect, because when we mounted the stairs the hands of the clock on the main landing stood at no more than fifteen minutes past the hour.

It was cold on deck and the few people about had sensibly put on coats and scarves. We walked to the dull roar of the ship as it waded the leaden sea. The night was moonless, windless; rags of dance music floated up from the deck below. 'It's parky,' I exclaimed, the word rising from my subconscious like a fish from the deep.

'A curious adjective,' Scurra pondered. 'It can mean both inclement weather and a sharpness of tongue. It's intriguing, don't you agree, the flotsam we allow to surface from the past?'

'The toy horse remains submerged,' I said.

We continued our walk in silence; it was too cold to stand at the rail. I had the feeling Scurra was abstracted and tried to think of an interesting topic for discussion, something that would return his thoughts to me. I wondered if it would be impolite to ask what advice he had given Bruce Ismay all those years ago.

'I've been mulling over our conversation of yesterday,' I said at last, 'with regards to the division of capital. Perhaps I was wrong ... there is always another way ...'

'Dear God,' he groaned. 'How easy it is to shake convictions.'

'All I meant,' I protested, 'is that possibly I would be better employed in fighting inequalities from a position of strength. Some of comrade Tuohy's ideas ... I approve of them, of course ... I mean, they're sound enough in theory ...'

'But it might be more advantageous to join the system rather than oppose it,' Scurra prompted.

I nodded.

'From the highest of motives, of course.'

'Yes, indeed –'

'No doubt you plan to improve working conditions. Perhaps you envisage recreational halls, cricket pavilions –'

'Yes,' I replied enthusiastically. 'Yes, exactly,' though until that moment such things hadn't crossed my mind. A vision of a garden city came into my head – thatched cottages, a hospital, playing fields, a cemetery with angels spreading plaster wings above tended graves.

'If you ever did get that far,' Scurra retorted, 'you'd be damned disappointed at the outcome. It would soon be brought home to you that the profit motive, which you now consider so venal, is no more than common sense –'

'Never,' I cried out.

'After you've paid for the doctor's surgery ... the school ... naturally, you'll want to endow an orphanage ... and the buildings have become fixed in time ... the planting of ivy against the foundations is of great help in the fostering of this deceit ... you'll come face to face with ingratitude ... hostility even ... murmurings of discontent amongst the very people you've endeavoured to help. Inevitably there'll be a demand for higher wages ... and why not, seeing it will have become apparent to all that you have money to burn –'

'It won't be like that,' I shouted.

'At best your generosity will be thought of as patronising and at worst no more than a rich man's attempt to enter the kingdom of heaven. A reasonable assumption, don't you think?'

'I don't believe in heaven,' I muttered. 'Only justice.'

He was still chuckling when a figure emerged from the underhang of the life-boats. It was Riley. He thanked me, belatedly, for the tip I had sent him via McKinlay. 'Civil of you, sir,' he said, 'but then, you're a real gentleman.' The sarcasm was illconcealed.

Scurra asked if it was true we wouldn't now dock in New York until Wednesday morning. 'I gather our speed is below what was expected,' he said. Riley replied this was so. He wasn't sure whether it was on account of conserving coal or because the ship had logged six ice warnings in the last twenty-four hours.

We went indoors shortly afterwards. The bone above my eye had begun to throb. Scurra's handshake was not quite steady when we parted for the night. I put it down to the cold.

FOUR

Saturday, 13th April

It was something Rosenfelder said, and the diatribe that followed, that further brought home to me the confusion of my life and necessity for change. I had known it all along, of course, but had decided time or circumstance, such as my experiences in Belfast, would nudge it into order. It was as though the tailor had prior knowledge of the disaster about to overtake me.

At daybreak I had woken feeling distinctly uneasy. I had slept without dreams or none that I remembered, yet something troubled me. After mulling over the events of the previous day I reasoned it was no more than to be expected considering the turmoil of my thoughts since meeting Scurra. I dressed and went up on deck. The sun had climbed above the slate-flat sea and streaked the sky with rose. It was bitterly cold and deadly calm; even the huge ship beneath my feet seemed but a plank of driftwood inert upon the unfathomable depths of that vast and silent ocean. I felt more uneasy than ever, which made me melancholy. Thinking that exercise would cure me, I went down to the swimming baths and found Rosenfelder kicking his heels in the passageway. We were forced to wait until the attendant arrived with keys a half-hour later.

The conversation turned to Scurra and the attraction he held for us. He was such a stimulating fellow, deep without being obscure, cultured yet devoid of cant. Neither of us were sure of his profession. I plumped for his being a lawyer but conceded that with his range of acquaintances and his knowledge of pictures, economics and politics he could be any one of a number of things. We remembered the way he had so adroitly dealt with Adele's fainting fit. Possibly he was a medical man, and then again he might be the proprietor of a newspaper. Rosenfelder had seen him dining with Mr Stead in the à la carte restaurant.

It was after we had swum three or four lengths and were temporarily beached on the tiled steps, Rosenfelder exhaling like a whale, that I remembered the several explanations given for Scurra's scarred mouth.

'That first time we spoke,' I said, 'when you took hold of my arm and asked who Scurra was … you seemed to think he'd been in a duel.'

'So he had. It accounts for his lip.'

'He told me he was bitten by a parrot in South Africa. And Archie Ginsberg thinks it was a blow from a rifle.'

'Bird, gun … who cares?' said Rosenfelder. 'It makes for interest,' and he plunged into the water and sank upright, the bulge of his bathing cap bobbing like a lily-pad. Thrashing to the surface again, he asked, 'The people you mix with … you find them amusing?'

'Some more so than others.'

It was then he said, 'Does it not occur to you that none of them are normal?'

At first I put up a defence, mostly because I feared I was included in their number, but soon fell silent. Nothing he said could be disputed. My friends, he argued, were not

living in the proper world. Their wealth, their poorly nur-
tured childhoods, their narrow education, their lack of
morals separated them from reality. Some, those with more
intelligence, might struggle to break away, and succeed for
a short time, but in the end, like the action of a boomerang,
it was inevitable they would return to the starting point.

'Then there's little hope for me,' I said.

'You are different. You have a conscience. The others will
remain perched on a dunghill of money piled up by those
who climbed out of the gutters of Europe.'

'You sound like Scurra,' I told him.

'I sound like any man who is no longer young,' he retorted. 'They are unworthy companions. I advise you to
remove yourself from their influence. Among better people,
you may find happiness.'

We didn't breakfast together. Mrs Duff was taking him to
meet Mr Harris, the theatrical producer. I didn't bother
going back to my room but went straight into the restaurant.
I was full of good intentions. Wallis was there with Ida and
they called me to sit with them. Rosenfelder hadn't mentioned women among his list of undesirables. No sooner
had I done so than Wallis leaned across and smoothed the
damp hair back from my forehead. It was an intimate gesture, not in the least motherly. Then, drooping a little in her
chair, she confessed to feeling sad.

'Why?' I asked.

'Because you go out of your way to avoid me, Morgan.
Which is a pity since I so enjoy being with you.' She
sounded absolutely sincere. She was wearing a blue dress
fastened at the shoulder by a glass button which she played

with while continuing to gaze at me steadfastly; she didn't once look away to the door. The expression in her eyes could best be described as both fond and subservient.

I didn't believe I was fooling myself. Even dear old Ida appeared conscious of undertones; I knew she didn't take sugar yet twice she stirred her tea so violently that it slopped into the saucer. I didn't give in immediately; Wallis had raised my hopes before and dashed them just as quickly.

'I was feeling pretty blue myself earlier on,' I said. 'It's so empty out there.' I looked towards the windows that cut the now bright day into squares of glittering light; already I could scarcely remember why the world had seemed so dark.

Wallis said, 'It's confusing, isn't it? We long to go home and once there ache to get away.'

'But to what?' I countered. Talking to Wallis was not unlike sparring with Scurra. It occurred to me that he'd infected the ship.

'In your case,' she said, 'I imagine you have it mapped out,' and again she touched me, this time the merest brush of her fingertips against the bruised skin above my eye.

'If I've been avoiding you,' I lied, 'it's because I have a lot on my mind. My future … that sort of thing. It's different for you girls.'

'Different, certainly,' she replied, 'yet no less hard. Not unless, like Sissy, one falls into marriage.'

'Not falls,' I protested. 'It was a love match.'

She said she was glad to hear it and that I must have felt lonely once Sissy had gone off with Whitney and set up an establishment of her own. We had always been so close. It couldn't be easy for me living with my aunt … now that she was deaf and often out of her mind.

'I love my aunt,' I said stiffly, 'and have any number of friends. Too many, I often think.' I didn't need Wallis to feel sorry for me and found her reference to my aunt's nervous disposition offensive, that is until I remembered the cross she bore on her own mad mother's behalf. It's true, I thought. We are none of us normal.

'Hopper complains I avoid him too,' I told her. 'I guess I'm a fair-weather friend.' She appeared to think this over, staring at me still and twirling that glass button round and round. Poor Ida didn't know where to put herself; she started to hum Adele's aria of the night before.

'We played a game at tea the other day,' Wallis said. 'Hopper, Charlie, Archie Ginsberg, the usual crowd. Who would one choose to throw out of a balloon if it was in danger of crashing?'

'I thought it was an open boat in danger of sinking –'

'It's the same principle,' she said. 'You'd be surprised who was the first to go.'

'It's a cruel game,' I said. 'And I expect it was Ginsberg.'

'No,' cried Ida. 'It was Charlie. He was quite upset. We did choose Ginsberg but then he told us he knew all about balloons and that he was the one person likely to get us down safely.'

'Ida went next,' Wallis said. 'Then you.'

'Me,' I exclaimed, and tried not to sound surprised.

'Yes, you,' she said. 'Because we all agreed you wouldn't bother to argue your case. You wouldn't, would you?'

I shrugged and admitted it was probably so. 'Do you suppose,' I asked, 'that if one went up in a balloon the earth would appear to drop rather than the balloon to lift?'

'You don't have much in common with Van Hopper, do you?' said Wallis. 'Or with Charlie? You don't skim the surface.'

It was the second time that morning I had been singled out as different. It rather went to my head, though naturally I protested I was a fairly average sort of fellow. She would have none of it. In her opinion I was special. I had a quality of aloofness both tantalising and touching.

'Tantalising?' I said.

'Yes,' she said. 'Very.'

Needless to say I picked at my food and was beside myself with excitement. It was obvious I had only to say the word and she would consent to an assignation. I shall dream no more, I thought, crushing my toast into fragments.

Presently, time having flown and it now being ten o'clock, she and Ida got up to leave. They were going to the Turkish baths. Wallis peered into the Gladstone bag she was holding and sat down again, 'Oh dear, silly me,' she wailed, 'I've forgotten my bathing-robe.' Prettily she asked to borrow mine; it was, after all, too utterly tiring trekking back along all those corridors.

'I only have my dressing-gown,' I said. 'And it's still rather wet.'

'What does that matter?' she replied. It can be imagined with what alacrity I handed it to her.

I spent a good part of the morning in the writing room

going over my letter of the previous day. Impulsively I added the line *I long for our union* and crossed it out moments later, fearing it sounded too much like a proposal of marriage. It was not wedded bliss I was after. Lest such a reckless sentence could still be deciphered I overlaid it with the word 'apple' written out five times. It was something Sissy had taught me when I'd once crayoned a lavatorial phrase on the day nursery wall and found it wouldn't rub off; the loops of ls and ps obscure anything. I would have used a fresh piece of notepaper if I hadn't felt the drop of blood beneath my signature counted for something.

The morning lasted for ever. At least half a dozen times I went and hung about the doors of the elevator in hopes of seeing Wallis, and for an hour I waited in my stateroom anticipating her knock at the door, a seductive smile curving her moist lips, my damp dressing-gown on her arm.

She was in neither of the dining saloons at luncheon. Hopper said he'd seen her playing quoits earlier with Charlie Melchett and Mrs Carter. I had a drink with him and Rosenfelder in the smoke-room bar and talked gibberish. Rosenfelder was bucked because he'd shown Mr Harris a sketch of the dress Adele would eventually model and he'd pronounced it damn fine.

'And so it is,' I cried. 'It's the most beautiful dress in the world.'

'You have not set eyes on it,' said Rosenfelder. They both looked at me strangely. I longed to confide in them but couldn't trust Hopper to keep his mouth shut; I didn't want Ginsberg sniggering at me for the rest of the voyage.

I don't know how I got through the afternoon. I was

happy, impatient, terrified by turns. I drank quite a lot, of course, and penned a ridiculous letter to my uncle telling him I intended to follow in his footsteps and make him proud of me. *I do not forget,* I wrote, *that but for the love you bore your first wife, I would possibly be toiling in a cotton mill in Lancashire.* Fortunately I was not too far gone to tear it up before I dozed off at the writing table.

I was jerked awake by Ginsberg's hand on my shoulder. He looked at me with concern and asked if I was feeling unwell.

'On the contrary,' I told him. 'I've never felt better. What is the time?'

'You don't look it –'

'I've been drinking,' I cried impatiently. 'Has it gone six o'clock?'

'By ten minutes,' he said, at which I rose unsteadily to my feet and rushed from the room.

There was just time to bathe my face and brush my hair before delivering the note to Wallis. If all went well it wouldn't matter that I wasn't dressed for dinner; food would be the last thing on our minds. And if it went badly and she turned me down – why then, I would throw myself overboard.

That wretched steward, McKinlay, did his best to delay me, rambling on about some absurd rumour he'd heard concerning George Dodge. 'Young Mr Dodge, sir,' he said, 'has threatened Mr Ginsberg with the hiding of his life for upsetting his sister.'

'Young Mr Dodge,' I retorted, 'would find it difficult to

swat a fly, let alone engage in a punch-up. I advise you to stop listening to gossip.'

Heart thudding, I reached A deck and approached Wallis's stateroom. As luck would have it people were changing for dinner and the corridor was deserted. I knelt, thrust the note under her door and ran back the way I had come. In my head I saw her sitting at her dressing table, tweaking a glossy strand of hair more fetchingly into place. In a moment she would rise, walk into the next room and catch that gleam of white on the floor. Now she was adjusting a fold in her dress ... taking those few short steps into my life ... she was picking up the envelope, tearing it open, smoothing out that creased sheet of paper with the rusted splodge below my name. She was frowning. 'Oh God,' I cried out loud, and bursting through the doors into the foyer came face to face with her.

I've no doubt my reaction was wild enough. For some seconds I thought time had accelerated, that she was on her way to our assignation; I actually seized her in my arms. I came to my senses when she beat at me with her fists. Appalled, I let her go. She said coldly, 'Morgan, I suggest you drink several cups of black coffee. I shall pretend this never happened. It would be best, don't you agree?' and walked away towards the doors of the library.

I don't remember going back to her room. For all I knew I might have travelled by balloon, for the earth had given way beneath me. I did have the cunning to knock at the door in case Ida was there. When I entered I could smell lavender water. The envelope rested like a diminutive doormat on the carpet. Snatching it up I crossed into the bedroom. It was in darkness but the light from the sitting room illuminated Wallis's dress flung upon the counterpane of the bed. There were buttoned shoes to match, poking from the frill of the valance. My velvet dressing-gown lay in a crumpled heap in the shadows of the half-open door. Standing there, noting the glimmer of the powder bowl on the dressing table, the shimmer of silk stockings draped across the knob of the wardrobe, I heard the door open and close in the room beyond.

Wallis said, 'Hurry.' Her voice was uneven, as though she'd been running.

Scurra said, 'My dear, you know I never hurry such things.'

*

I grew old cowering in the shadows of that room reeking of lavender. In spite of the ghastly nature of my predicament – any moment I might be discovered – I burned with a jealousy so fierce that I had to clench my jaws to keep my teeth from grinding. Not that I would have been heard. How foolishly I had deceived myself in thinking that I desired nothing more than a casual intrigue of the sort often described by more fortunate men – for now, listening to those voices which rose and fell and started up again with horrid definition, I shuddered with revulsion. It wasn't the words themselves that shocked me – *I want your lovely prick*, nor his reply – *Show me your lovely cunt*, but the context in which they were used. Such expressions belonged to anger, mockery, contempt; how foul they

150

sounded when linked to the making of love. I guess I was out of my senses for a time, or rather wholly under the sway of more primitive ones, for I shamelessly pressed myself against the jamb of the door and timed my groans with theirs. It was over for me quicker than for them, and I was left, a blind voyeur, scrabbling for memories to blot out the continuing din of their beastly coupling.

My aunt took me to Italy to visit the crater of Vesuvius when I was eleven years old. We travelled to the summit on the funicular railway. From the station platform one glimpsed through cloud the curve of the shore at Naples, the sea and the city gleaming in a net of gold thrown by the setting sun. A seven course dinner, served before we set off, was included in the price of the ticket. It began with soup and a rack of lamb and ended with ice-cream. The dining compartment was loud with the noise of champing and swallowing. I furled my tongue round the lump of ice in my glass of lemonade and sucked it small. *Tie me, said Wallis*. The train was worked by ropes which owing to the extreme tension creaked alarmingly as we climbed by fits and starts, the outline of the mountain edge running parallel to our course. The angle of inclination began at forty degrees, increased to sixty-three and decreased again as we gained the upper station. Alighting in the fiery darkness we passed through a gate punched in a wall of lava and walked higher. *Not so fast, said Scurra*. One of our group was foolish enough to pick up a blackened cinder that rolled beneath his boot. He was a gentleman, yet the stream of obscenities that issued from his anguished mouth set the women in the party trembling. Till then the rim of the old crater had stood

151

between us and the new eruptive cone, but as we left the ash-strewn path a glow of burning light riveted us to the spot. Suddenly, preceded by a sound which is impossible to describe – something like an almighty blast of wind in the naked branches of a winter forest, or the fall of a crested wave on a shingled beach – millions of glowing particles, from the size of a cannon-ball down to a tiny spark, spattered the air and erected a fretwork of fire across the black heavens. The smell of sulphur made me catch my breath.

Scurra said, 'Well, that was very satisfactory, don't you think?'

Wallis said, 'I want to die.' Their laughter swilled round the room.

Soon after, they left. I emerged on all fours like an animal, nose sniffing the unnatural odour that stung the air. They hadn't bothered to plump up the cushions, nor remove the length of cord, now uncoiled like a snake, dangling from the back of the sofa. I entered the bathroom and with a square of wet soap wrote *fuck* on the glass above the basin. Then I returned to my stateroom and slammed the door.

My feelings of humiliation, rage even, were as nothing compared to the relief I felt at having escaped without being exposed. I shook at the thought of what might have happened if they had tired of the sofa and staggered to the bedroom. I could hardly have pretended I was inspecting the plumbing. There were three whole days left in which I would meet them daily, exchange pleasantries, drink with them. In their company I would surely act like a man demented, their secret lodged in my breast like a gun primed to blow my heart to pieces. How I hated him! How I wished her dead – and on the thought understood Adele's smile of radiant grief. Fists clenched, the blood pounding in my ears, I paced the room. I couldn't get out of my mind that length of cord on the sofa. I saw it duplicated in the hang of the undrawn curtains across the porthole, the electric wire protruding from the desk lamp. Looking wildly about I caught my mother's painted eyes gazing at me from the wall. Tearing the portrait off its hook I rushed into the passageway and up on to the boat deck. On the way I roughly brushed against Mrs Straus, who, on the arm of her husband, was tottering down the turkey runner of the Grand Staircase. Mr Straus rounded on me angrily and, blundering lout that I'd become I raced on regardless.

I don't know whether I really intended to throw the painting of my mother into the waves. True, I wanted to cast her from me. It was she, not the fetid old woman who counted gold each night, who had bound my wrists with string and tied me to the iron bolt of those half-closed shutters overlooking that stinking worm of water. Shivering in the icy air I leaned over the rail and on the instant was seized from behind.

Scurra's voice said, 'No, Morgan. No.' He spun me round. I couldn't read the expression in his eyes because the lamp-light glittered on his spectacles, but for once he no longer smiled and the set of his riven mouth, so lewdly employed but twenty minutes before, was grimly purposeful.

He wouldn't let go of me, though I tried to shake him off. 'No,' he said again, and tightened his grip. I believe he thought it was myself I wanted to be rid of.

153

'It was cruel of you,' I shouted. 'It was you who encour-aged me to approach her.'

'My life has gone in a flash,' he said. 'As yours will.'

'Words,' I crowed. 'Just words.'

'How else are we to be understood?' he demanded.

'I loved her,' I whined. 'I wanted to please her.'

'We have but a short time to please the living,' he said. 'And all eternity to love the dead,' and with that he prised the painting from my grasp and rubbed at her face with his sleeve. 'Come inside,' he implored. 'There's a good chap. It's cold out here.'

'You had no right,' I muttered. 'It was not the behaviour of a friend.'

'My dear boy,' he said. 'Have you not yet learnt that it's every man for himself?'

FIVE

Sunday, 14th April

Nothing lasts, neither joy nor despair. Having retired to bed considerably the worse for drink and hoping to die, I woke refreshed and full of optimism. Memories of the latter part of the previous night eluded me, though I remembered telling someone – either Hopper or Charlie – of my amorous encounter with Wallis in the foyer and receiving an assurance that when next we met she would behave as if nothing had happened. Indeed, I seemed to recall standing near her in the elevator when I was taken up to clear my head, and she was smiling; this was probably wishful thinking. As for the earlier half of that momentous evening, beyond a slight twinge of guilt at having smeared that obscene verb on the bathroom glass, I'd banished the whole shameful business from my mind and resolved never to dwell on it again. Here, Sissy came once more to the rescue – she'd taught me long ago that if ever a frightening picture flew into my head I was to imagine a giant foot coming down to stamp it flat.

When McKinlay came in with the tea he unaccountably carried the painting of my mother under his arm. He said an affable gentleman in spectacles had given it to him first thing that morning. He made to replace it on the wall but I told him to leave it propped against the skirting board.

'I hear we won't be docking now until Wednesday morning,' I said.

'That was the case yesterday, sir. I understand our speed has increased since then and we might yet make it by Tuesday night. Of course, it's not an easy matter to berth a ship of this size in darkness.'

'I suppose not.'

'But Captain Smith's the man to do it, sir. I've sailed with him four times on the *Olympic* and believe me it's an education to see him con the ship at full speed up the channels entering New York. There was one particular time, very tricky it was, sir … it could have ended badly. It made one flush with pride the way he swung her round, judging his distances to a nicety, she heeling over to the helm with only a matter of feet to spare between each end of the ship and the banks, and him standing cool as a cucumber with his wee dog at his side.'

'I've noticed he doesn't drink,' I said. 'Not even wine with his dinner.'

'Not a drop, sir. But then, a man with drink in him is mostly out of control.' I thought he looked at me too boldly and was about to remind him that he hadn't been too steady on his pins the other afternoon when there was a knock at the door. It was Charlie, at which McKinlay, gathering my clothes up from the floor and holding them ostentatiously at arm's length, left.

Charlie had come expecting to find me prostrate. 'You were terribly squiffy last night,' he said. 'And morose. You kept wishing you were dead. Several times you came out with the most appalling language. Fortunately the girls weren't present.'

'Who brought me back here?'

'The Jew with the curls. The one Mrs Morgan's taken a shine to. He and I took you up on deck. You were frightfully sick. That's probably why you look so well now.'

'I feel brand new,' I said, and meant it. 'From now on I'm going to be as dull as ditch water and turn my life around. You're talking to a serious man.'

'You had cause,' he said. 'It must have been horrid for you, Wallis ticking you off and all.' At this I started to think of the *all* and quickly summoned up the image of that giant foot.

'If you really are going to be dull,' he went on, 'perhaps you'd spend the morning with me. They're holding a church service in the saloon at ten.' He stared at me so earnestly and so humbly I could have hugged him. 'Dear, sweet Charlie,' I replied, 'I can think of nothing more exciting.' At this, even his nose flushed pink.

Captain Smith conducted Divine Service. Passengers from all classes attended, those from the third fairly gawping to find themselves in such opulent surroundings. They were sent to stand at the front which was a mercy because some of the children smelled and many scratched their heads continuously. I couldn't see Adele, but then, for her, a visit to the top decks hardly ranked as a novelty. Nor was Wallis present. I'd half hoped she would be, thinking she'd be less inclined to give me the cold shoulder in the middle of a religious service. Then again, it would ill suit her to adopt a holier than thou attitude when only a few hours before – here, I brought that foot down sharp.

Smith read the service from the company's own prayer book. It didn't seem all that different from the *Book of Common Prayer* except it appeared to go on longer. The orchestra accompanied the hymn singing. Charlie sang his head off. The cellist got an attack of hiccups; every time his chest jerked his bow bounced on the strings. My shoulders started to shake but Melchett shot me such a look of reproach that I checked myself. The only thing that kept me awake was the kerfuffle that broke out when a strapping woman from steerage belted a boy round the ear for fidgeting and he kicked her back. That and the singing of 'Eternal Father Strong To Save'. Hearing those ragged voices begin the ascending plea, *O hear us when we cry to Thee for those in peril on the sea*, it was hard to remain unmoved. One or two ladies, overcome with emotion, audibly sniffed. I was idly studying the elaborate plasterwork of the ceiling when I became aware that someone at the front had turned round to look at me. It was Mrs Straus's maid, who had once worked for Sissy. Instantly I remembered my disgraceful behaviour on the stairs.

As soon as the service was over I went in search of Mr and Mrs Straus, running them to earth in the Palm Court. They accepted my apology kindly enough. Mrs Straus said she couldn't be cross with me this morning of all mornings, or anyone else for that matter, because she and Mr Straus anticipated communicating by wireless telegraphy with their son and his wife who were on their way to Europe on board the passing ship *Amerika*. She hadn't the least notion

160

of how such miracles were performed but was grateful they could be accomplished on her behalf. I asked Mr Straus if he'd been approached by a Mr Rosenfelder who was intending to visit Macy's in the coming week. He said he hadn't but if I would point him out the next time we were in the lounge he would willingly have a word with him.

Feeling virtuous I rejoined Melchett and spent a very dull half-hour indeed reading in the library. Or rather Charlie read. Every book I dipped into seemed to carry some sentence or other that reminded me of the night before. I had the steward scurrying up and down the library steps like a squirrel hastening to gather nuts before winter set in.

Finally I told Charlie I was in need of exercise and emerged on deck in time to hear the mighty hooting of the ship's whistles, which, in accordance with company rules, required testing in mid-voyage. Sextants in hand, the ship's officers crowded along the wing of the navigating deck, shooting the sun and calculating our position in the ocean. They wore their greatcoats for it was noticeable how far the temperature had dropped since yesterday. The sea was as black as coal, the white avenue in our wake pointing its arrow-head at the pale horizon. I was about to return indoors to fetch my own coat when Thomas Andrews, hatless and wearing a beautifully cut suit of dark blue serge, caught up with me and asked if he could have a quiet word. Oblivious of the cold and the continuing boom of the whistles he said he and his team had been monitoring the use of the writing room and were convinced that though it was extremely popular with the ladies it was over-large. It would be no more than commercial common-sense to reduce its size and convert the extra space into first class accommodation. Bearing in mind my satisfactory work as a draughtsman and knowing that my uncle wanted me to have more settled employment, he wondered if I would be interested in drawing up plans for such a project. It would afford both of us the opportunity to find out what I was capable of, though, of course, he couldn't promise that any finished design would be used. He didn't want me to answer yes or no at this moment. Would I come to his suite at two o'clock precisely?

I really did think God had taken a hand in my affairs. Overjoyed, I hastened to collect measuring tape, pencil and paper and raced to the writing room. I had forgotten all about Wallis, or rather the ticklish situation existing between us, so much so that when I saw her sitting there, alone, I waved my hand quite naturally and smiled. She smiled back. She looked pale and I noticed the uneven texture of her complexion. It would be going too far to call her skin blotchy, yet nevertheless it was not as smooth as I remembered. When she spoke I was struck by the thinness of her lips and the peg-like appearance of her teeth. It was as though always before I had glimpsed her through a mist, which had now cleared, revealing imperfections.

'You look happy,' she said.

'I am,' I replied, and busied myself taking measurements. Shortly after, she gathered up her things and left.

The writing room was certainly spacious enough to be reduced in size, but I was worried by the extent of the alterations necessary, bearing in mind plumbing and electrical considerations. One half of the room had an almost perfect reproduction of a Georgian ceiling with the most exquisite carving and moulding which would either have to be sliced in two and modified or else taken down altogether. Mrs Brown of Denver was at an alcove table, playing Patience. Observing me stalking about the room she asked if I was thinking of buying the place. We both laughed.

It was wonderful to feel in such high spirits, to know in what direction my life was going. I would never drink again, or at least not to excess, nor waste my time with the likes of Hopper or George Dodge. Even dear old Charlie, being far too indolent, would have to be left behind. I was going to become a naval architect or an interior designer, possibly both. After all, Andrews had managed this double feat. One day I would stride round some great Atlantic liner, a team of draughtsmen trotting at my heels, carefully jotting down my every suggestion.

I was brought back to earth by Ginsberg, who poked his head round the door and announced that the noon to noon speed had just been posted up in the smoke-room and it was the best day's run yet, 546 miles. 'Are you prepared to place a bet?' he asked, to which I loftily replied that I was not a gambling man. 'You surprise me,' he retorted. 'You definitely were last night. You'd have lost your shirt if Melchett hadn't stepped in.'

*

At two o'clock on the dot I knocked at the door of Andrews' suite. His sitting room resembled an office with plans of various sections of the ship pinned to the oak panelling of the walls. The table and chairs had been pushed back to accommodate an enormous drawing desk, behind which he sat with his sleeves rolled up to the elbows. He waved me to sit. Propped on the mantel above the fireplace stood a framed square of writing with the last line underscored in ink. He kept me waiting a good five minutes before looking up from his work.

He didn't ask for my decision; I reckon he knew that I would jump at the chance. Instead he told me how his own career had begun at Harland and Wolff. His first three months were spent in the joiners' shop, the month after with the cabinet-makers, the one following working in ships. Then a further three months in the main store; five with the shipwrights, two in the moulding loft, two with the painters, eight with the iron shipwrights, six with the fitters, three with the pattern-makers, eight with the smiths. A spell of eighteen months in the drawing sheds completed his five years as an apprentice.

I must admit my heart sank at this litany of hard labour. There was worse to come. He had undergone a rigorous course of night studies in order to gain a knowledge of machine and freehand drawing, applied mechanics and the theory of naval architecture. He had read until his eyeballs seemed to have been rolled in sand. Soon after his twentieth birthday he was given the supervision of construction work on the *Mystic*, represented the firm at the trials of the *Gothic*, went to Liverpool to report on the damage done to the *Lycia* and helped in the renovation of the *Germanic*. 'If you wish to succeed, Morgan,' he said, 'you must think while others sleep, read while others play.'

'I will,' I said. 'I will. I want to. I've already thought of a way of converting part of the writing room while conserving certain features. It should be possible to –' but before I could explain fully we were interrupted by an urgent knocking.

He went out into the vestibule and opened the door to Bruce Ismay. I couldn't hear every word they said. Ismay seemed to be complaining that the ship wasn't going fast enough. Smith had apparently had the ship's course altered earlier that morning. We were now slightly to the south and west of the normal course which would result in further delay.

I got up to read that framed writing on the mantel-shelf. If it was a prayer it was pretty self-congratulatory.

Of all who live, I am the one by whom
This work can best be done in my own way.
Then shall I see it not too great nor small,
To suit my spirit and to prove my powers.
Then shall I cheerfully greet the labouring hours,
And cheerful turn, when the long shadows fall
At eventide, to play, and love, and rest,
Because I know for me my work is best.

It was the last four words that had been underlined.

I heard Andrews say, 'You yourself showed me a wireless message from the Greek steamer *Athenai* reporting large quantities of field ice in latitude 41° 51 north and longitude 52° west.'

'There's always ice at this time of year,' Ismay said.

'Damn it all, this is a maiden voyage,' and then both voices grew heated. I gathered they were arguing about the importance of arriving Tuesday rather than Wednesday.

'Take it up with Smith,' Andrews shouted. 'He's in command,' and with that there was a muffled grunt from Ismay and the door banged shut behind him.

Andrews returned looking irritated. He sat down at his desk and took up his pencil. He appeared to have forgotten I was there.

'The writing room –' I began.

'You'll find the relevant plans on the sideboard in the vestibule,' he said. 'I imagine you'll find it convenient to work *in situ*,' and with that I was dismissed.

I surprised myself with the quantity of work I managed to get done before tea-time. I had in mind a structure similar to a stage set, rooms within an existing room, complete with false ceilings. In this way it would not be necessary to tear down the main ceiling or damage the splendid panels inlaid with mother of pearl that graced the writing room. The scheme had the added advantage of being relatively simple to dismantle should the time come when the original space needed to be restored. I felt this might well come about sooner than expected; according to the steward the ship was already a quarter empty of first class passengers.

At five o'clock I went in search of Scurra and Rosenfelder. I wanted to tell them what I'd been doing. Scurra, in particular, would surely be pleased at my new-found sense of purpose. In the event, only Rosenfelder was in the smoke-room and he was too selfishly pre-occupied, on account of Adele wearing his gown that evening, to listen. He did, however, inform me that I'd tried to scramble out of the porthole last night when he'd escorted me to my room. 'That's all in the past,' I said, 'because I know for me my work is best.' I proved it by drinking nothing but a glass of lemonade. The mood I was in it tasted like champagne.

I did meet Scurra before dinner, on A deck, where I'd gone in hopes of seeing Riley. For some unfathomable reason I needed to make my peace with the young seaman; it irked that he held me in contempt. On Rosenfelder's behalf, Scurra had been below to visit Adele. 'He's anxious to make sure,' he said, 'that she intends to keep her promise.'

'And does she?'

'Without a doubt. Not a word to Rosenfelder, but I've crossed her palm with silver.' He asked if the steward had returned the painting to me. I thanked him, then blurted out, 'Mr Andrews wants me to design something for the ship. It's to do with the writing room. There's no guarantee that my work will be used, but it's a start, isn't it?'

'It is indeed,' he said enthusiastically. 'I'm delighted for you. And if you succeed, which I don't doubt, you will have killed two birds with one stone.'

'In what way?'

'An honest day's wage for an honest day's work. You can build your hospitals and schools with untainted money. There is a difference, don't you agree, when it comes to profit, between Commerce and Art?' I think he was being sincere.

'Rosenfelder has equally bright hopes for the future,' I said. 'That's good too, isn't it?' It was important he should think I was interested in someone other than myself. He agreed and mentioned that Wallis and her sister Ida had arranged for Adele to change for dinner in their room. Before I could stop myself, I asked, 'Are you in love with Wallis Ellery?'

He turned to me in astonishment, black eyebrows raised above his spectacles. 'Love?' he barked. 'Good heavens! Love is what women feel.'

*

Molly Dodge had forgiven Ginsberg; George and he had shaken hands on it. That was the hot news in the lounge before dinner. Kitty Webb told me. Apparently it was only half an apology, because though he'd declared he was sorry for insulting the memory of Molly's mother, he refused to withdraw one word in regard to the Germans. In fact he'd referred to them as beasts all over again. 'One has to admire his pig-headedness,' Kitty said. 'After all, he's of German stock himself.'

She asked how I was feeling. Had I got myself together? She didn't care what people thought about my friends ... they were just a load of dead beats, but it mattered that I was getting quite a reputation.

'A reputation for what?'

'For acting wild. I know you weren't involved in that scuffle in the dining saloon, but old man Straus was blowing steam over you knocking Mrs Straus down the stairs.'

'I did no such thing,' I protested. 'I merely jogged her arm.'

'Of course, but these things get worse in the telling. And

last night Benny claims you caused such a rumpus in the smoke-room you had to be removed.'

'I was upset,' I muttered. 'Something happened earlier –'

'It sure did,' she said. 'You assaulted Wallis Ellery.' I was about to sulk when she flashed the smile of an angel and tapped my knee gleefully with her blunt little nails. 'Serves her right,' she crowed. 'I've never understood what you boys see in her. She's flat-chested and she's a prude.'

'You're possibly right,' I said, though I was only speaking of Wallis's chest.

'You'd be far better off making a play for Molly, or even Ida. But then, I shouldn't think you want to get married.'

'Not yet,' I said. 'Do you?'

'Not yet,' she replied evenly, 'but I will one day … when Benny's wife tells him it's time to stop.'

She was very frank. She said it was much better being the mistress of a rich man than a poor one, and it had nothing to do with money. Well, obviously it had … what she meant was that if Guggenheim had been earning a few dollars a week and living in a cold water apartment, his having a girl on the side would be darn selfish.

'And unlikely,' I said. 'Unless it was true love.'

'Jesus,' she exclaimed. 'There's nothing true about love.' My expression must have conveyed dismay, for she again playfully tapped my knee. 'Take my word for it, Morgan, there wouldn't be any joy in it, not after the first flush … all those meetings on street corners … all that petting in dark doorways with the rain pelting down. The wife would soon cotton on and give him hell … make him feel like a rat –'

'It's a dismal picture,' I said.

169

'If you're rich, nobody gets hurt. Who can accuse Benny of neglecting his family?' There were other advantages too. For instance, if a man was next to broke his woman was called a floozie; if well-heeled, a secretary.

'Or a gold-digger,' I said.

'Yes,' she said, 'but not to their face.'

We both watched the snail-like progress of Mr and Mrs Straus through the doorway. As usual, they were arm in arm. The way they leaned together it seemed that if either one let go the other would lose balance. I couldn't be sure whether I found this touching or disturbing. Such dependence was surely dangerous. If one of them got detached, what then?

Ginsberg arrived shortly after with Hopper. They'd been messing about in the gymnasium. They had intended to jog round the deck but the cold was enough to freeze them in their tracks. There wasn't a breath of wind, the sea like glass, and the stars – 'I've never seen such a starry sky,' Hopper enthused, 'not even in the desert.'

Ginsberg congratulated me on becoming a protégé of Thomas Andrews. He sounded genuinely delighted, which threw me. I noticed Hopper kept quiet. Ginsberg had heard the news from Rosenfelder, though in the telling I'd turned into the designer of a new ship of the White Star line, one possibly larger than the *Titanic*.

'It's just a few drawings,' I corrected. 'And there's not the remotest chance of their being used. I guess it's a sort of examination.' Hopper looked relieved. Ginsberg insisted on drinks all round, by way of celebration. Thinking it churlish to refuse, I was careful to take small sips. By the time the bugle blew for dinner Hopper and he were on their second bottle.

Wallis came late to our table. She'd been helping Adele get dressed; Ida was still engaged in the titivating. Wallis sat next to me. I didn't turn a hair, nor did I need to call up the giant's foot, not even when she took out her handkerchief and I caught the scent of lavender. What had happened was no more than a photograph snapped long ago, in another country, its chemical impression now fading. I even had the composure to apologise for my behaviour in the foyer, though it was somewhat tongue in cheek. 'You must have been very frightened,' I said. 'It was the action of a brute.'

'I've forgotten it,' she answered graciously. 'As must you. By the way, your dressing-gown is being laundered. You shall have it tomorrow.'

The soup was being served when Rosenfelder's moment came. Several times I'd glimpsed his tubby countenance at the glass, anxiously peering to see if the dining room was full. He'd obviously squared it with the orchestra and arranged some kind of signal, for suddenly the waltz song from *The Merry Widow* petered out and the pianist thumped a cadenza. Conversation straggled to a halt. Lady Duff Gordon rose to her feet and pointed with her fan towards the doors, at which the violinist raised his bow and the haunting opening notes of 'One Fine Day' stole through the hushed saloon. Adele entered on the arm of Rosenfelder.

It doesn't matter that I'm not qualified to judge what she wore or that I couldn't even describe it adequately – none of us men could, beyond it was shaped like an hour-glass and made of some kind of silk that picked up points of dancing light – for Adele and the dress were one, and as she advanced, the splendid column of her neck circled with borrowed diamonds, those pearl-pale eyes with their strange expression of exaltation fixed straight ahead, we held our breath in the presence of a goddess. For a fleeting instant I saw her as Joan of Arc prepared for battle, the bodice of her generous bosom sheathed in silver. A little flood of material swished behind her as she marched; flipping it expertly to one side she rounded the Duff Gordons' table and stood waiting to be seated. It was Mr Harris, not Rosenfelder, who pulled out her chair.

I was pleased for the tailor; he was not just a flash in the pan. Nor was Adele. The two would rise together. There were some, Hopper for one, who thought the whole caboodle smacked of vulgarity. Nor could he think what we saw in Adele. She was pretty enough, but far too tall for a woman. And where the devil did she go to after her spectacular appearances?

'No, she wouldn't do for you,' drawled Wallis. 'But then, you're on the small side, aren't you?'

The dinner dragged on. If anything, not drinking was having an hallucinatory effect on me. I had the curious impression I was part of a group seen from without. I had to go on eating because if I looked up I might see faces pressed to the window, hands clawing the glass. The noise too was outside, a dull intermingle of shrieking voices and clattering china. And there was another sound, a high-pitched whistle such as the sand at Singing Beach gave off when stepped upon. I turned, opened my mouth to tell Molly Dodge I thought of the North Shore near her home,

172

but she wasn't there. Ginsberg was slicing a peach in two, preparing to gouge out the stone with his knife. He glanced up and the reflection of the candles leapt in his eyes. The table tilted. The next thing I remember I was in the outer room, crouched on a wicker chair, Hopper pushing my head down between my knees, a lump of ice melting on the back of my neck.

Ida said it was the heat. All the windows were tightly closed because of the intense cold outside. She tugged my head up and prised out the stud of my collar. I jerked like a rabbit in a trap as the sliver of ice slid further down my spine. Hopper was worried about the clout he'd dealt me with his racquet. In Melchett's opinion it was a delayed reaction to my excessive drinking of the night before; judging by the disdainful glance bestowed on me by Mrs Carter, just then leaving the restaurant with Mrs Brown, it could be reckoned I was in the middle of a repeat performance. That good old sport Mrs Brown winked as she passed by.

I recovered quickly enough, physically, that is, feeling no longer sick and being quite steady on my feet. Mentally, something was wrong. As I walked to the smoke-room, Hopper and Melchett at either elbow and Ida faffing along behind in case I took another turn, I distinctly heard voices uttering sentences that didn't finish. *An hour and a half. Possibly ... Hadn't we better cancel that ... As we have lived, so will we ... If you'll get the hell out of the ...* I shook my head to get rid of them and they trailed off like mist pushed by the wind. Once in the smoke-room, Hopper urged me to down a small measure of medicinal brandy, which made me shudder. As soon as I could I got away from him, insisting

I needed to go out on deck, alone. I promised I'd be back in a jiff, and if I wasn't he should come in search of me.

He was right about the cold; the air stung my lungs. I was about to dodge back inside when I saw Riley sauntering towards the companionway up to the officers' house. I called out his name, clapping my hands together to keep them warm. When he'd come close enough, I said, 'Look here, I want to explain myself.'

'Is that so?' he replied. 'And why would that be?' He stood there, his face sinister in the lantern light, breath steaming.

'I'm not sure,' I said, and I wasn't. 'Something bothers me. Can't we talk?'

He said, 'That we can't, sir. Piss off,' and with that he turned his back on me, cool as you please. I was astounded at his insolence.

Melchett, Hopper and I played bridge later on, Ginsberg making up a fourth. We were mostly abstemious because Astor was sitting at the next table with Archie Butt, military aide to President Taft. I sat very straight in my chair; beyond a glass of hot lemonade I drank nothing and hoped it was noted. Butt was trying to find out from Colonel Astor, who had apparently recently been skiing in St Moritz, what the 'Cresta' had been like this year. He was having a hard time of it getting Astor to respond, he being his usual gloomy self and looking as though he'd just come from a funeral. Eventually Astor said he hadn't the faintest idea, his bride having persuaded him from the run for fear he broke a leg. He wasn't such a stuffed shirt as I make him out. He'd invented a brake for bicycles and even written a book. Sissy had actually read it; it had something to do with melting the Arctic to put the world on an even keel. He became more animated when the name Kitty was mentioned. I pricked up my ears, as they say, but the Kitty in question turned out to have four legs; she was an Airedale belonging to Astor, off her food and tied up aft of F deck.

Butt and he left at half-past eleven. I know that because Butt took out his watch and expressed surprise at the lateness of the hour. I guess he was desperate to get to his bed. They had been gone no more than ten minutes – Ginsberg had ordered a whisky and Charlie and I had just won three tricks in succession – when suddenly the room juddered; the lights flickered and Ginsberg's cigarette case, which sat at his elbow, jolted to the floor. It was the sound accompanying the juddering that startled us, a long drawn-out tearing, like a vast length of calico slowly ripping apart. Melchett said, 'We're in collision with another ship,' and with that we threw down our cards, ran to the doors, sprinted through the Palm Court and out on to the deck. A voice called, 'We've bumped an iceberg – there it goes,' but though I peered into the darkness I could see nothing. From somewhere forward we heard laughter, voices excitedly shouting. Coming to the starboard rail I looked down on to the well of the third class recreation area; there were chunks of ice spilling and sliding in every direction, all shapes and sizes, glittering under the light of the foremast. Steerage passengers, most in their ragged night-clothes, were chucking it at each other as though playing snowballs. Hopper raced off to go down there and join in the fun. Charlie and I found it too cold to linger and hurried back indoors. A

175

dozen or so men had poured out of the smoke-room and were milling about the foyer, pestering the stewards for information. Astor was there, still dressed but without his tie, leaning down to shout into the ear of Seefax who had been woken from sleep in the library and now sat on the staircase with his stick raised like a weapon. Everyone had a different explanation for whatever it was that had jarred the ship; Ginsberg swore we had lost a propeller, but what did he know?

We couldn't resume our game until Hopper returned, which he did quite soon, triumphantly carrying a lump of ice in his handkerchief. He thrust it under my nose and it smelt rank, a bit like a sliver of rotten mackerel. He dropped it into Ginsberg's whisky when the poor devil wasn't looking.

We must have played for another ten minutes, by which time Hopper said he'd had enough. Remembering Andrews' injunction that I should read while others slept, I decided to spend an hour in the library. I was crossing the foyer when the man himself swept past on his way to the stairs. I didn't think he'd seen me but he said quite distinctly, 'Follow me. You may be needed.'

He led me up to the navigating bridge. Captain Smith was evidently expecting him because as we approached the wheelhouse the quartermaster flung open the door. I would have followed on Andrews' heels but he shouted over his shoulder that I was to wait outside. Through the glass panels I could see Smith and his first and second officers clustering about him. Ismay was there too, dressed in a fur

coat and wearing carpet slippers. He seemed to be ex-
cluded, roaming up and down, hands in pockets.

I was glad I wasn't outdoors, for even in the comparative
warmth of the bridge house I found myself shivering. The
silence wrapped me like a cloak and it was only then that I
realised the ship no longer moved. When I pressed my face
to the window to look down at the sea there was nothing but
darkness; when I tilted my head the blackness was fiery
with stars.

Soon, the group inside, all but the quartermaster, came
out and walked straight past me. I followed at a distance,
unsure of my position, and then Andrews doubled back
and told me to put on warm clothes and return to the bridge
as soon as possible.

There were even more people in the foyer when I made
my way down. It was an incongruous sight; the mixture of
clothing, the dressing-gowns and bathing-robes worn with
gloves and scarves and fur tippets, the women with their
hair loose, the men with their naked throats and ankles the
colour of lard. I didn't recognise Lady Duff Gordon until I
heard her voice. She had creamed her face for sleep and her
eyebrows had disappeared. No one seemed particularly
disturbed by what had happened. The laughter bubbled
beneath the drifting cigar smoke.

I put my tweed jacket on over my evening clothes and
then my Newmarket coat. I thought of wearing my cap – it
matched the tweed – but when I tried it on in the mirror it
made me look too young. I hadn't the faintest notion what
Andrews expected of me. As a precaution I stuffed an exercise book into my pocket along with several pencils, in case

I was asked to patrol the decks and jot down details of steamer chairs snapped by the shower of ice. McKinlay met me in the passageway. He'd been off duty but now everyone was on call. Not that there was anything to worry about. We'd start engines any moment. I went back to the bridge and waited.

I couldn't tell anything from their expressions when they returned. Ismay wasn't with them. This time as they passed through the door Andrews indicated I should follow. I stood respectfully at a distance beside a notice board on which ice warnings were pinned like butterflies.

The talk was fairly technical. The water had risen approximately fourteen feet about the keel, forward. The watertight bulkhead between boiler rooms 6 and 5 extended only as high as E deck. The first five compartments were filling and the weight of the water had already begun to pull her down at the bow. When it sank lower the water from Number 6 boiler room would swamp Number 5 boiler room. This would drag the bow even lower and water would flood Number 4, Number 3, Number 2, and so on.

'How long have we?' asked Captain Smith.

Andrews snapped his fingers at me and I dug out my pencil and exercise book. I was dreadfully afraid it was I who would have to make the calculations, but it was just paper he wanted. Once only he glanced up at the clock above the door. It was two minutes to midnight.

'An hour and a half,' he said, at last. 'Possibly two. Not much longer.'

SIX

Monday, 15th April

There is no way of knowing how one will react to danger until faced with it. Nor can we know what capacity we have for nobility and self-sacrifice unless something happens to rouse such conceits into activity. In the nature of things, simply because I had survived without lasting hurt, I remembered little of those other occasions on which I'd been in considerable peril, once half-way up Mount Solaro when I'd been foolish enough to climb on to a wall and lost my footing, the other when tumbling from the side of a boat negotiating the Suez canal. Besides, I had been a boy then and it had been my own lack of sense that had landed me in trouble. As I trailed Thomas Andrews to his suite I confess I fairly glowed with exhilaration and can only suppose I'd failed to grasp the full import of that exchange in the wheelhouse. Andrews hadn't uttered a word to me since leaving the bridge; now, coming within a few paces of his door, he turned and said, 'They'll be lowering the life-boats shortly and will need extra hands. Take nothing with you save what can be put in your pockets. Avoid alarming people. Tell the truth only to those among your friends who can be relied upon to keep a cool head. Have you a pocket knife?'

'I have,' I said.

'Keep it with you,' and with that he went inside.

The crowd had dispersed when I crossed back through the foyer. Most of the men had returned to the smoke-room bar; judging by the noise they were in boisterous mood. Ginsberg and Melchett were at our old table, Ginsberg occupied in building a house out of the pack of bridge cards. This surprised me. I had thought he'd be in the thick of it, spouting his opinions about a lost propeller to all and sundry. I sat down feeling important.

'Look here,' I began, 'I think it would be best if we went out to give a hand with the life-boats. Most of the crew will be needed for other things.'

'You've experience of davits and such like, have you?' asked Ginsberg. 'I mean you've been through the drill?'

'Well, no ... but –'

'Then you'll be a lot of use, won't you?'

'We won't actually be getting into the boats,' scoffed Hopper. 'It won't come to that. Why, the women would never stand for it. It's too cold.'

I said, 'I happen to know that it's more serious than you think. I have it on the best authority that things are looking pretty bad. There isn't a great deal of time.'

'Time for what?' Hopper asked.

'For us to get into the boats,' I said. 'It's essential we put on more clothes.'

'I think not,' Ginsberg said. 'I doubt we'll be getting into any boats, not unless the clothing you have in mind includes petticoats.' He was still playing with his house of cards, his tongue caught between his teeth with the effort of laying on the roof. Hopper looked mystified. There'd been a time, years ago, when I too had gone out of my way to baffle him.

'Look here,' I shouted, 'this isn't a game, you know.' I tugged at Ginsberg's elbow to make him listen and sent his cards in a heap.

'How many boats did you say there were?' he asked.

'I didn't,' I retorted. 'But as a matter of fact there are sixteen, plus four collapsibles.'

'Capable of carrying how many? Fifty at the most?'

'More like sixty,' I snapped.

'And how many of us would you estimate are on board?' He was watching me through half-closed eyes, waiting. A burst of laughter came from the direction of the bar. A voice began to bellow the 'Eton Boating Song'. What a fool I am, I thought, and the elation which had buoyed me up drained away and I was left swirling the cards round and round on the table-top in imitation of a whirlpool to stop my hands from shaking.

Just then Rosenfelder rushed in, his expression deeply gloomy. As always, he was looking for Scurra. A steward had come into the Palm Court, where he and Adele had been drinking high-balls with the Duff Gordons, and ordered them to their quarters to put on life-preservers before going up on deck. They had asked what luggage they'd be required to take with them and been told they couldn't take anything, nothing but the clothes they stood up in. What was he going to do about his dress? He wasn't allowed to carry it in its box and it was unthinkable that Adele should wear it in a life-boat. 'There is the oil,' he wailed, 'the dirt, the salt-spray ... it will be ruined. Where is Scurra? He will use his influence. Where are his rooms?'

None of us could tell him. Hopper had seen him in the

passageways of both A and C decks. Ginsberg had bumped into him along the main corridor of B deck, but he could have been coming from anywhere. Rosenfelder looked at me. 'I've not been to his room,' I told him. 'My steward hasn't even heard of him.'

'Then he's one in a million,' said Hopper.

'Why not ask Wallis Ellery,' Ginsberg said. I noticed his voice was unsteady. He seemed to be having difficulty with his breathing. I fancied he was more alarmed than he let on.

'She is not to be found either,' Rosenfelder moaned. 'Adele's clothes are in her room. I have knocked at her door but there is no reply.'

At that moment the bar steward came over and politely asked us to leave. We must all go as quickly as possible to fetch our life-preservers and assemble on deck. There was no cause for panic. It was simply a precaution. I arranged with Hopper that we meet in the gymnasium in ten minutes. 'We'll stick together, won't we,' he insisted. 'It'll be like the old days.' 'Yes,' I assured him. Ginsberg strolled into the foyer and lowered himself into a leather armchair. Rosenfelder panted up the Grand Staircase in search of Scurra. Before we parted, Hopper touched my arm, 'You're my oldest friend,' he murmured, 'and my best.' His eyes were scared. Ginsberg looked up and waved sardonically as the doors of the elevator clanged shut; he was holding a handkerchief to his nostrils.

I rode below in the company of two ladies in wrappers and a man wearing pyjamas beneath a golfing jacket. I swear the stouter of the women was the one who had expressed disappointment at there not being more of a show when we left Southampton. She was going to the purser's office to withdraw her valuables from the safe. Not that they amounted to much. She had a watch left to her by a grandmother born in Kent, England, a diamond pin that had belonged to her dead mother and an album of family photographs. If it came to the pinch, she said, she'd choose the album every time. The steward had told her to fetch what small items she had because everyone might have to get into the boats. The man in the golfing jacket laughed and said this was highly unlikely. 'I'm not entirely sure,' he said, 'this isn't some elaborate hoax. After all, the ship is unsinkable.'

When I entered the passage McKinlay and the night steward were knocking on doors, urging people to go up on deck. I felt curiously detached and had the notion I swaggered rather than walked; I'd never been so conscious of how good it was be young, for I knew it was my youthful resolution as well as my strong arms that would enable me to survive the next two hours. I thought of old man Seefax and his feeble grasp on life and reckoned he might perish from nothing more than lack of hope. By now, wireless messages would have been dispatched to every vessel in the area, and even if there wasn't enough room for all in the boats, there would still be time for those left behind to switch from one ship to another. Somewhere in my mind I pored over an illustration, in a child's book of heroic deeds, of a rescue at sea, ropes slung between two heaving decks and men swinging like gibbons above the foaming waves. How Sissy would gasp when I recounted my story! How my aunt would throw up her hands when I shouted the details of my midnight adventure! Why, as long as I wrapped up well it would be the greatest fun in the world.

Accordingly, having reached my stateroom, I put my cricket pullover on under my jacket and taking off my dancing pumps struggled into three pairs of thick stockings. I had to pull one pair off again because I couldn't fit into my boots. Then I went into the corridor and got McKinlay to help tie the strings of my life-preserver. He jokingly remarked that I'd put on weight since we last met and asked if I had with me everything I wanted to take. He'd been instructed to lock all the doors until the emergency was over – in case things went missing. They were having a spot of trouble keeping the steerage class from surging up from below.

'I'm working for Mr Andrews,' I told him. 'I may need my room as a base … to write reports … that sort of rigmarole.'

'It's orders, sir,' he said.

'Well, in my case, just forget them, there's a good chap.' He hesitated, but the 'good chap' did the trick and he left my door alone. On an impulse I went back inside and took up the painting of my mother. Taking out my knife I levered the picture from its frame, tore out the stretchers and rolling up the canvas stuck it in my pocket.

There were now a dozen or more people filing in procession towards the elevator. They were mostly pretty cheerful, engaging in banter to do with each other's quaint attire. A gentleman carrying a top hat and wearing tennis shoes beneath a coat with an astrakhan collar was much admired. He said he thought his hat would come in useful if baling-out was required. One woman cradled a Pekinese dog with the snuffles, another a pink china pig.

I decided to go below to see for myself what was happening. Descending the stairs I was aware of there being something not quite right about the slope of them. They looked perfectly level but my step was slightly off balance; my feet didn't seem to know where to land, and I was tilting forward. I put it down to imagination, that and the bulky clothing which encumbered me, and marvelled that Rosenfelder must feel this propulsion all the time.

I didn't get very far. There were too many people streaming in an opposite direction. On F deck an officer barred my way. He was holding on to the arm of a steerage woman who was carrying a baby against her cheek. The officer tried to restrain her and turn me back at the same time. 'Why have we stopped?' she kept asking. 'What for have we stopped?' Behind the officer's shoulders I saw a line of postal clerks at the bend of the companionway, heaving mail sacks, one to the other, up from the lower level. The sacks were stained to the seals with damp.

Retracing my steps I made my way upwards again. On the staircase landing of C deck I passed White, the racquets professional. He didn't acknowledge me though I raised my hand in greeting. From somewhere along the corridor a voice called out, 'Hadn't we better cancel that appointment for tomorrow morning?' I didn't hear White's reply.

Colonel Astor was in the foyer talking to Bruce Ismay. Ismay had the appearance of a man on his death bed; his face had become as old as time. Owing to the numbers thronging the stairs I was prevented from going immedi-

187

ately up top and heard Astor say, 'Is it essential I bring my wife on deck? Her condition is delicate,' and Ismay's response, 'You must fetch her at once. The ship is torn to pieces below but she won't sink if her bulkheads hold.'

There was a fearful crush in the gymnasium, spilling out on deck and flowing in again as the cold stabbed to the bone. Hopper was nowhere to be seen. Mrs Brown jogged my sleeve and asked if it would be a good idea to start community singing, but before I could answer the far door was thrust open and the ship's band struck up something jolly. Kitty Webb sat astride one of the mechanical bicycles. She wore silk pyjamas under a man's leather automobile coat and was accompanied by Guggenheim's valet. I went out in search of Hopper. Save for a solitary man gripping the rail there was no one about under that glorious panoply of stars. I imagined the crew must be all assembled at the stern; before quitting the wheelhouse I had heard Captain Smith's call for all hands on deck.

I was walking towards the port side when suddenly the night was rendered hideous by a tremendous blast of steam escaping from the safety valves of the pipes fore and aft of the funnels. I clapped my palms over my ears under the onslaught and turned giddy, for the noise was like a thousand locomotives thundering through a culvert. Even the stars seemed to shake. Recovering, I spied Hopper watching an officer attempting to parley with the bridge above. The officer was pointing at the life-boats and soundlessly roaring for instructions. Hopper and I, bent double under the din, ran back inside.

The crowd in the gymnasium had mostly retreated to the

landing of the Grand Staircase and the foyer beneath. The band was now playing rag-time. Kitty Webb, head lolling like a doll, danced with Mrs Brown. Mrs Carter asked if Captain Smith was on the boat deck and whether I knew the whereabouts of Mr Ismay. I said I expected they were both on the bridge seeing to things. There was such a dearth of information, of confirmation or denial of rumours – the racquets court was under water but not the Turkish baths; a spur of the iceberg had ripped the ship from one end to the other but the crew was fully equipped to make good the damage and were even now putting it to rights – and such an absence of persons in authority to whom one might turn that it was possible to imagine the man in the golfing jacket had spoken no more than the truth when presupposing we were victims of a hoax. In part, this lack of communication was due to the awesome size of the wounded ship. It was simply not possible to keep everyone abreast of events. An accident at the summit of a mountain is hardly observable from the slopes. For the rest, what was Smith expected to do? Should he appear on the landing of the Grand Staircase beneath that rococo clock whose hands now stood at twenty-five to one in the morning and announce that in spite of the watertight compartments, the indestructible bulkheads, the unimaginable technology, the unthinkable was in process and his unsinkable vessel, now doomed, unfortunately carried insufficient life-boats to accommo-date all on board?

Ginsberg was still in his armchair opposite the elevator, still clutching a handkerchief to his nose. An unknown girl was chatting to him; he introduced her but the loudness of the band blotted out her name. She had an enormous expanse of brow, beneath which her features sat truncated like those of an infant's; it was possibly on account of her hair being dragged back in a fearsome bun. She said, without preamble, that she had known for several years past, from dreams and such like, that it was her destiny to drown. She spoke of it quite calmly and without resorting to melodrama. Her doctor had dismissed her condition as no more than nerves; her mother had enrolled her in the local tennis club, in the hopes that strenuous exercise in the fresh air would banish such fancies. She had become quite exceptionally adroit on the courts, but the dreams persisted.

'There is nothing to worry about,' I said. 'I myself have been plagued by nightmares. I'm convinced they consist of memories of the past rather than portents of the future.'

Ginsberg was leaning back in his chair, breathing like a man recovering from a record-breaking run round the tracks. Hopper asked what was wrong and he explained he was afflicted with asthma. It came on sometimes without reason. His handkerchief was smeared with a concoction of honey obtained from a bee-keeper in a Shaker community in Massachusetts and would do the trick shortly. I thought it was an inspired excuse and fancied he was in a blue funk.

It was then that I realised I hadn't seen Charlie Melchett since the interruption to our game of bridge. In Hopper's opinion it was probable he'd galloped off to play knight errant to the Ellery sisters and Molly Dodge. I made my excuses to the girl with the forehead and went looking for him. Lady Melchett, but six weeks before, had drawn me to one side and entreated me to keep an eye on her boy. 'He is

so very fond of you,' she'd said. 'He looks up to you.' 'You
may rely on me,' I'd told her, fighting off those damn dogs
threatening to lick my face away.

I ran him to earth quite quickly, standing in the deserted
gymnasium gazing out at the shadowy deck. The funnels
continued intermittently to release those deafening blasts of
steam and though the sound was muted by the glass I had
to shout to draw his attention. He didn't turn round. 'Why
does it keep on with that ghastly noise?' he asked.

'It's a bit like a train,' I said.

'I thought I saw a ship out there a few minutes ago.'

'I expect it's coming to assist us.'

'No,' he said. 'It's stopped moving. Perhaps it's just starlight.'

'You ought to fetch your life-preserver,' I said. 'I've got
mine on.'

'I will ... soon. I needed to mull things over. I should have
liked –' The gush of steam started up again; when it had
died away he was still rabbiting on and I reckoned he was
speaking of his father – '... I know he's fond of me but it
worries him how I'll face up to things when he's gone. I'm
not brainy and I don't often think of anything downright
important. My mother dotes on me, and that's rather held
me back. I've never had to go it alone, not like some chaps.
Not that I'd want to. I'm no good on my own ... I lack
common-sense.'

'Charlie,' I protested, 'you have more common-sense
than any man I know ... and kindness and a generous heart
–'

'I would have so liked to make him proud.'

191

'Hopper and I are in the foyer,' I told him. 'We rather wanted you with us.'

'I'll come and join you in a bit,' he said. I hesitated, but felt it my duty to ask, 'You're not frightened are you, Charlie? There's no need to be.'

'There's nothing on this earth that frightens me,' he said. 'It's what comes after that concerns one. I've not always behaved decently.' His voice wobbled. I couldn't help smiling. If the worst happens, I thought, God will surely send all his angels to bring Charlie to heaven. 'You'll have plenty of time to atone,' I said, 'a life-time, in fact,' and at that he faced me and, sheepishly grinning, followed me down the stairs.

Ida and Rosenfelder hurried to meet us. Neither of them could find Wallis. Ida had looked for her everywhere, asked everyone if they recalled seeing her, but nobody had. 'She was in the dining room when I got back after your faint,' she babbled, 'but then I went off to a concert in the second class lounge and later I had coffee with Molly in the Café Parisien … then that dreadful bump came and Molly said it was safer to remain where we were. Mr Rosenfelder's been awfully kind. He went to our room but it's locked, in case of looting or something, and the steward shooed him away.'

'I knock and knock,' Rosenfelder said. 'And I think I hear voices, but there is no one opening and the steward tells me I have no business in that passage.'

I offered to go there again, just to set Ida's mind at rest, and walked away in a deceptively leisurely manner. Once out of sight I fairly sprinted. The corridors of A deck were deserted, as though this was an ordinary night and all good folk were abed. I didn't attempt to knock on Wallis's door;

192

instead I sought out the steward and demanded he hand over the key. He refused, saying it was more than his job was worth. I told him I would break the door down, if necessary, to which he retorted he would report me to the chief steward. I shouted he could report me to Captain Smith for all I cared, and we glowered at one another for some moments. 'Listen,' I said. 'I have reason to believe that Miss Ellery is in there with a gentleman friend. This sort of thing can't be new to you. Naturally, when you first knocked she thought it would compromise her to respond. She possibly waited until she believed you'd gone away, only to find the door locked. You take my meaning?'

'Perfectly, sir,' he said. 'Why didn't you tell me that in the first place?' Taking the key off its ring he planted it in my hand. I told him to make himself scarce, which he did, beetling off down the passageway no doubt eager to inform the second steward of the salacious goings-on. I turned the lock, slipped the key under the door and ran for the companionway. I had no wish to confront Scurra.

*

In the short space of time I'd been absent, the atmosphere in the foyer had undergone a change. Some course of action had at last been resolved upon; there was a sense of relief rather than urgency as the stewards moved discreetly from one group to another, urging the women to proceed to the top deck. Ida refused to budge an inch without her sister until I said I'd go with her, mark where

193

she was and bring Wallis to her side the moment she was found. I assured her it wouldn't be long.

The chief saloon steward led us by way of the crew's narrow companionway up to the forward boat deck. Colonel Astor and his bride, the Carters, the Theyers and Mrs Hogeboom went ahead, slowed down by the stately progress of Mr and Mrs Straus, linked as always. Hedged by Hopper and Charlie I held tight to Ida's hand. Mrs Brown's grandchild, riding his father's shoulders, bobbed above our heads blowing on a tin whistle. There was even some laughter as we squeezed upwards. Behind, abreast with Lady Duff Gordon, nudged Rosenfelder, clad in a fur coat the colour of beeswax.

Captain Smith appeared at the top, waiting agitatedly to descend. Astor asked him a question, something to do with how the situation now stood, and he answered stoutly enough that all was under control, but we must hurry. We emerged on to the bridge, a little below the officers' house, and were told to wait. Thankfully, the steam pipes remained silent. A stir was caused by Mr Theyer excitedly pointing to what he took to be the lights of a ship to the right of our stern. We watched intently but the lights receded and we came to the conclusion we were confused by starlight.

Some of the men, myself included, climbed down the companionway, starboard side, to be closer to the boats in case we were needed. There were very few seamen about and only two officers, both grappling with the complicated machinery of the davits. We called out that we were willing to assist but they waved us away. The night was perfectly still, save for our footfalls, the low murmur of voices and the crackle of canvas as the boat covers were trampled over. Astor paced alone, the tiny glow of his cigarette arching through the air as he flung it overboard. I remember Charlie talked to me about cricket. Above, a million stars sprinkled the heavens.

Some fifteen minutes later, nothing having been accomplished on our part of the deck, Hopper and I went round to the port side. Here, we saw one boat, free of its tackle, being lowered towards the rail. Suddenly there was a flash of light from the forward deck, a hissing whoosh sufficient to turn the stomach over as a rocket soared to meet the stars. Up, up it went, and we craned our heads to watch it go, until, exploding with a report that tore the night in two, illuminating for one stark instant the fretwork of wires upon the tapering mast, it sent its own stars sailing down. The women and children on the bridge clapped their hands in wonder at the pretty sight; we men could scarce look at one another, recognising it for a desperate measure.

Mrs Brown's voice floated down from the bridge, 'I wish you would make up your minds. We were told to come up here,' and at that the crowd began to move inside again. Hopper and I hurried through the gymnasium doors and made our way below to meet them.

Jerkily, the boats were being lowered alongside the windows of the enclosed promenade of A deck. Someone had to fetch a chisel to crank up the glass. Mr Carter said the list of the ship had meant the boats hung too far out from the top rail for the women to enter safely. An officer thrust steamer chairs through the windows; when the nearest boat was level, he climbed out, one foot on the chair, one foot on the gunwale. There was no panic or undue excitement until he ordered the men to stand back from the women and children. Then, several of the women began to blub. Mr Carter challenged him, at which he bellowed, 'Women and children first.'

To a man we obeyed him. Ida clung to my arm, whimpering Wallis's name, but I shook her off and gave her into the charge of Mrs Brown. A young woman carrying a baby refused to leave her husband, but he said she ought because of the child. 'There's nothing to worry about,' he told her. 'I'll be on the next boat, sure thing.' Mrs Straus was being led to the window when she stopped and said, 'I'm not going without Mr Straus.' Someone, Theyer I think, asked the officer if an exception couldn't be made for such a revered and elderly man? Whereupon, Straus turned away, remarking he would not take advantage of his age. Mrs Straus, dragged a further few steps, broke free and stumbled to his side. 'We shall stay together, old dear,' she said. 'As we have lived, so will we die.' This remark, though noble in sentiment, convinced the woman with the baby that she was parting from her own husband for ever. Shrieking, she attempted to clamber out of the boat and was pushed back by the officer. The infant set up a thin howl. Mr and Mrs Straus strolled a little way off and sat in steamer chairs, watching the proceedings as though from the stalls of a theatre.

Remembering my promise, I went inside to look for Wallis. I passed through the swing doors, propped open to the night, to that landing from which an eternity ago Madame Butterfly had glimpsed a ship on the far horizon. The or-

196

chestra stood there now, playing for the benefit of those outside. They had assembled in a hurry; I could see the score in the carpet where the cellist had dragged up his instrument.

Scurra sat below in the Palm Court, sprawled at a table with his legs stretched out. He was discussing the Peloponnesian War with Stead, the journalist. Neither of them took any notice of me. Mr Stead was neatly dressed for a windy morning on Wall Street. His life-preserver lay draped across his knee. Scurra wore a long black overcoat beneath which dangled the hem of my purple dressing-gown.

I was forced to interrupt their conversation. 'Look here,' I said, 'it's important I find Wallis. Ida won't get into the boats without her.'

'She's somewhere around,' Scurra said. 'She was rather tied up when the call came.'

I couldn't fight him. I slumped into a chair and fought my own demons, calculating in my head how long I might survive in that icy water, should it come to it, while Scurra debated whether Thucydides' account of the destruction of the Athenian fleet was truthful or not. He dwelt particularly on the drowning incidents, arguing that as the Greeks were half fish by nature and as the temperature of the sea off the harbour was generally high, it was surprising so many had perished. My mind drifted, until I swam with Hopper in that lazy lake at Warm Springs.

Presently, the journalist stood and shook us both by the hand. 'It's been an interesting trip,' he observed. 'I doubt we'll see another one like it.'

'Quite,' said Scurra.

When Stead had gone, the room became deathly quiet. Save for a man at a table in the far corner, a full bottle of Gordon's gin at his elbow, we were alone. The orchestra had decamped to the deck outside. Scurra appeared lost in thought; one finger tapped at his gouged lip. The silence lay like a weight. Clearing my throat, I considered asking how he had really come by his scarred mouth, then changed my mind. For all it mattered, God himself could have taken a bite out of him.

At last, Scurra said, 'I was in the Turkish baths earlier. How very exhausting it is lying on an Egyptian couch with the perspiration collecting in the folds of one's belly. The only thing missing was a plate of grapes.' I didn't reply, knowing him for a liar; the baths were closed on a Sunday. He looked at me quizzically. 'You appear angry,' he said. 'Or is it your way of preparing for the ordeal to come?'

'Something like that,' I muttered.

'Apparently the liner *Carpathia* is on its way to us.'

'Is it?' My heart leapt in my breast.

'So Ismay tells me. Unfortunately she won't reach us in time.'

'I don't intend to throw in the towel,' I told him.

'I should think not. Still, it's curious, don't you think, how we cling to life when everything profound exhorts us to let go?'

'I'm not aware of it,' I said. I was tired of his philosophising. All I wanted was for Sissy to come through the swing doors and take me by the hand.

'Think of music,' he said. 'Why is it that we are most moved by those works composed in a minor key? Or disturbed to tears by the phrase ... "half in love with easeful death"?'

'I'm not,' I replied brusquely, and got to my feet.

'You mustn't worry about Wallis,' he called after me. 'She and Molly Dodge are in the care of Ginsberg. He took them up top ten minutes ago.'

On the promenade of A deck a handful of passengers strolled sedately back and forth. I was astonished to see Mrs Brown and Mrs Carter among them, having imagined they had got away some time before. Mrs Brown said it was over seventy feet down to the water and that the language used by one of the crew members was too foul to repeat. He had insisted on smoking, she said, and threw spent matches among them. She and Mrs Carter and young Mrs Astor had all got out again, though Ida had stayed. She'd attempted to clamber out, but her foot had caught in a rope. Mrs Carter had torn her coat prising herself through the window. It wasn't her best coat but she intended to sue the company when all this was over. The boat had been lowered only a quarter full. Mr Carter explained they were waiting for instructions to go further down into the ship. The second officer had ordered the gangway hatches to be opened so that they could enter the boats nearer the water. As yet, nobody had returned to fetch them. I asked why there were so few people about and was told that most preferred to hold on a little longer, seeing that the *Carpathia* was now steaming towards us.

I was making for the companionway to the upper deck when Rosenfelder approached. He urged me to come with him to find Adele who had gone to her cabin determined to rescue her Madame Butterfly costume. For some extraordinary reason he twice addressed me as lamb chop, once when we were rounding the landing on C deck and again when I made a wrong turning on level F. 'You are going backwards, lamb chop,' he scolded. 'Please concentrate.' I guess he was being affectionate.

There was terrible confusion below, the passageways jammed with people, their possessions stowed in pillow-cases slung across their shoulders. We saw not a single officer or steward as we forced our way through. A boy riding a home-made hobby horse with a skein of red yarn for a mane scraped my ankle; his mother scurried behind carrying an infant, a shawl over her breast, the tiny fingers of the child caught like a brooch in the wool. In the public lounge an untidy circle of men and women surrounded a priest reciting the rosary. Some knelt, others rocked backwards and forwards as though the ship rolled beneath them. The priest was a bear of a man with a great splodge of a nose and he gabbled rather than spoke, the responses swirling about him like the hectic buzzing of disturbed bees. Coming to a bend in the passage near the dormitories, we had to flatten ourselves against the tiled wall as a dozen or more stokers, faces black with grease and some carrying shovels, swept headlong past. The fans in the ceiling had stopped spinning and it was uncomfortably warm. I couldn't help contrasting this subterranean hell with the Eden above, where, under the twinkling stars, they paced to the swoon of violins.

Moments later we spotted Adele coming from the direction of the kitchens. One hand balanced aloft a cheap suitcase, a loaf of bread teetering on top, the other hitched up the skirt of Rosenfelder's dress, exposing her handsome legs to the knee. She wore a black cloak lent by Lady Duff Gordon; even so, we could clearly see the edges of that waterfall train had become trimmed with dirt.

'My God,' cried Rosenfelder. He pulled a handkerchief from the pocket of his honey-coloured fur and, sinking to the floor, frantically dabbed at the material. He was knocked sideways by the blundering run of a middle-aged man carrying a dinner plate rattling with spoons. I was ashamed on Rosenfelder's behalf – so much more was at stake than a ruined gown – and dragged him to his feet. Adele said, 'There's sea water trickling across the floor of the kitchen. My shoes have turned crusty,' and sure enough, her ivory slippers were stained yellow at the toes.

We escorted her to the boat deck, starboard. A boat was being prepared for lowering. Either the ropes were too new and too stiff or the cleats weren't oiled sufficiently, but the handlers were having a devil of a job getting her down from the davits. There was no sign of Ginsberg and the girls. Ascot and his wife were standing nearby, not touching, he looking out into the night, she drooping beneath the studded sky. He had brought up his dog; yawning, its breath curled like smoke. Mrs Brown was there too with the Carters and Mrs Hogeboom. Mrs Carter said she was worn out traipsing the stairs from one deck to another and would be glad to sit down. While we were waiting I strolled towards the stern. Ahead of me an officer hurried towards two women coming from the port side in the direction of the gate separating the first and second class. He held up his arm. 'May we pass?' one of the women asked, and he replied, 'No, madam, your boats are down on your own deck,' and they trailed away.

When our boat was at last ready and Mrs Carter had boarded, Mr Carter cried out, 'If anything should prevent me from following, everything you need to know is in the third drawer down in the bureau.'

'Yes, dear,' replied Mrs Carter.

The Astors stepped forward. Helping his wife over the gunwale Astor asked, 'I can go with her, can't I? She needs me.' His foot was raised, ready to climb. The officer replied, 'I'm afraid you can't, sir. We have to see to the women first.' 'I understand,' Astor said, and dropped back instantly. His wife looked at him; she gave a plucky little smile as he waved his farewell. I turned to Adele and seized her elbow. She was tearing chunks out of the loaf with her teeth, as though famished. She shook me away and crumbs flew in all directions. 'I'm not getting in that thing,' she said. 'I'll go when the Duff Gordons tell me it's time.' I think Rosenfelder was relieved at her refusal. Mrs Carter had shown him her torn coat.

The boat descended with creaks and groans. It was half full, no more. We peered down, waiting to hear it hit the water. 'We need a man,' bellowed the spunky Mrs Brown, her hat in the light of the portholes assuming the shape of a swooping vulture. 'There's no one at the tiller.' The officer shouted for a seaman and a wine steward from the à la carte restaurant darted forward and shimmied down the rope before anyone could stop him. Someone screamed out he was a damned scoundrel. We watched the boat row away.

There were no lanterns on board and once it had moved out of the shimmer of the porthole lights we heard only the ghostly splashings of the oars. 'Garfield has the key,' called Mr Carter. There was no reply.

The second boat was almost in place when it jammed some three feet above the rail. A complicated procedure required it to jerk upwards before coming down; I supposed this was to make sure the ropes were running free. The officer in charge turned – I was fortunate to be standing nearest to him – and called for assistance. I leapt at the chance, glad to be active at last, and put my whole heart into the task, tugging and pushing as though it was my own life that depended on it. And when we had got it straight, or fairly so, and the officer shouted for the women to come forward, I was able to help them up and tumble them aboard. Again the boat was cranked away half full, and I couldn't but do arithmetic in my head and subtract the saved from those left behind, particularly those bewildered souls I had seen below in the steerage class.

I was now ordered to the port side where there were more men than women gathered on deck. I learnt later that a rumour had gone round to the effect that men were to be taken off from here and women from the starboard side. Whatever the truth of it, when boat Number 5 was ready to be filled there were so few women that a dozen or more men were allowed to clamber in. I asked the officer if we shouldn't wait but he said there wasn't time and he daren't fill it to capacity, not at this height, because the boat might break in two under the strain. There are women and children waiting below at the gangway hatches,' he said. 'They can enter more easily from there.' As the boat dropped in fits and starts, the women clinging to each other, a commotion broke out to my right and a man shouted, 'Faster ... faster ... lower away faster, I tell you.' It was Bruce Ismay, whirling his arms round like a windmill. He had lost one of his slippers and his bare foot stamped the deck as he cried out again in a fever of impatience, 'Faster, damn you ... faster.' Then the officer supervising got angry, and shouted back, 'If you'll get the hell out of the way, I'll be able to do my job. You want me to lower away faster? You fool, you'll have me drown the lot of them.' At this Ismay limped off, his arms still swinging. I craned over the rail, expecting to see the boat halt on a level with the hatches, but it met the water and rowed away.

Shortly after, they started sending up more rockets, this time at five-minute intervals. As each glare flashed the deck with light the upturned faces froze in shock. In one such instant I glimpsed Adele, curved like a mermaid with that glimmering train swished aside. I made my way along the now crowded deck and reaching her, urged her to follow me. She told me she had arranged to meet up with Rosenfelder and the Duff Gordons on the forward area, but had lost them in a sudden stampede to starboard. I asked if she had seen Wallis and she said she had, in the foyer with Ginsberg and another girl, but that was a while ago. Wallis had been smoking a cigarette.

I was escorting her forward when an officer marched up and demanded I fetch blankets from the store room. Just then the Strauses passed by with their maid. The girl was crying, protesting that she didn't want to leave them, and they were assuring her that it was for the best and that she must think of her widowed mother. I pressed Mr Straus to look after Adele and he replied it would give him pleasure.

I hadn't the faintest idea where the store room might be, but remembering the rugs flung to the floor as they utilised the steamer chairs on the enclosed promenade, I hurried below. Securing a hefty pile I was about to return when I glanced through the windows into the smoke-room. It appeared empty save for a circle of men playing cards in front of the fire – but then, one of the players shifted and to my amazement, behind him in the alcove, I saw Wallis sitting with Ginsberg. Dreadfully concerned, I dashed inside.

When she saw me she waved her hand excitedly and cried out, 'Now we'll know what's happening.'

I could tell by their flushed faces that they'd both been drinking. Knowing what I knew about her, I suppose I shouldn't have been so shocked, but I was. Absurdly, I felt I was to blame in some way. Furiously I turned on Ginsberg and called him a blazing idiot for not taking her up on deck.

'Steady on,' he protested. 'I did try. She wouldn't have it.'

'I almost went,' she said. 'Earlier, with Molly. I feel rather guilty about it. She was clutching my arm and at the last moment I just twisted away. I couldn't stand the idea of being cooped up with all those bawling children.'

'Ida, at least, is safe,' I said.

'Safe?'

'Yes, safe,' I ground out. 'The ship is sinking, or hadn't you heard? She looked all over for you. The door to your room was locked.'

'I was with Ginsberg,' she insisted. 'I can't think why the door was locked.'

There was the slightest pause, in which she and Ginsberg exchanged glances. Defiantly, she took one of his cigarettes and waited for him to light it. 'Stay and have a drink,' she urged. 'The stewards have all vanished but Ginsberg keeps leaping over the bar.'

'You needn't look at me like that, Morgan,' Ginsberg said. 'I've been scrupulous in leaving money behind. It's as well to be honest, don't you think, even if no one will ever know.'

Tearing the cigarette from Wallis's fingers I crushed it flat in the spittoon.

'Dear me,' she cried, 'you're as touchy as Ida.'

'She didn't want to get into the boat,' I shouted, 'not without you. She would have stayed if the officer in charge hadn't shoved her aboard.'

'Poor dear Ida,' Wallis murmured, 'she's always responded to shoving,' at which, exasperated beyond endurance, I left them.

Guggenheim was blocking the gymnasium doorway, peering through the window to watch Kitty Webb walk away. He stepped aside to let me pass and Kitty looked back and called out, 'Be seeing you, Benny.' He said, 'Goodbye, little girl,' but I doubt if she heard because the door was already closing and the orchestra stood near by. In spite of the cold the cellist wore no gloves and I marvelled that he managed to hold his bow so steady on the strings.

Captain Smith had come down from the bridge and was standing with the quartermaster at the foot of the companionway. They were both staring into the night. I wanted

Smith to notice I was being useful, so I approached and handed the rugs to the quartermaster. He took them without comment; Smith's gaze never wavered from the horizon. It was possible to believe a whole fleet of ships lay anchored there, for the stars shone so brightly that where the heavens dipped to meet the sea it swam with points of diamond light. I walked further off, stamping my feet to stop my toes from freezing, until I heard the creaking of the davits on the forward area. They were releasing Number 1 boat and I raced to assist.

This time my help wasn't welcome; there were at least six or seven members of the crew manoeuvring it into position. Ready to shift, they all climbed in, and at that moment a man and three women crossed out of the shadows and I heard Duff Gordon's voice say, 'May we get into the boat?' and the rough reply, 'If you must.' I supposed two of the women to be Adele and the Strauses' maid, but as I got closer I saw both were elderly. I called out to Lady Duff Gordon, asking what had happened to Adele, but already the boat was swinging away and she couldn't have heard me. I shouted up to the officer to wait, for I had clearly seen there was room for thirty or more aboard, but he continued to work the ropes, bellowing at me to stand back; I guess he was under the impression that I was trying to save myself.

As the last life-boat on the starboard side dropped from sight, a great swoosh of smoke belched from the funnels and rubbed out the sky. When it had drifted on and the milky stars came back I heard the first gun-shot.

*

I was running in the direction of the report when Charlie came haring up.

'Wallis wants you,' he panted. 'You must come and talk to her. She refuses to move unless you speak to her. Hopper tried to carry her off bodily but she kicked him. She's frightfully squiffy.'

'The shot,' I said. 'I heard a shot.'

'There was a bit of a rumpus on the port side. Some of the men tried to rush the boats and the second officer fired over their heads. They were steerage passengers, of course.'

The men in the smoke-room were still playing cards. Ginsberg had gone. Hopper stood with his leg raised on a chair, scowling and rubbing at his shins. 'You talk sense into her,' he muttered. 'She's gone crazy.'

Wallis looked at me with glittering eyes. Such a look! Not crazy at all but ugly with suffering. I knew what was wrong with her without being told, as though her soul had flashed on mine. Pity welled up in me, and envy too, for I might never know the sort of love that gripped her by the throat.

'Please,' she croaked. 'I must speak to him. You will find him, won't you?'

'I'll try,' I said. 'But you must come on deck to be near the boats.'

'I can't move,' she said.

'I know,' I soothed. 'Charlie will carry you.'

I didn't look for Scurra. Not right away. There were more urgent matters to attend to, for when I came out on to the promenade there were at least a hundred people milling about the deck, shouting and shoving at each other in their attempts to get to a life-boat swaying at the rail. There were steerage passengers among them now; I caught sight of the priest with the nose and the boy with the hobby-horse. The officers were striking out with their feet at the men and hauling the women up like so many sacks. There was no thought in my mind of going back for Wallis; it would have been well-nigh impossible for Charlie to get her through such a crush. Hopper and I fought our way to the front and once there stood shoulder to shoulder, heaving the men aside and passing the women and children into the arms of the officer who knelt on the gunwale. Fists punched my face but I scarcely felt the blows.

This time there was no question of the boat going away half filled; seventy or more, mostly women, and some of those standing, made that lurching descent. They had almost reached the sea when something went wrong with the tackle and the ropes jammed – then she was nearly swamped by a jet of water propelled from the ship's waste pipe. A wail of terror gushed up. I had a good view of the whole desperate scene, for the moment the boat had begun to drop the crowd had fled further along the deck to where the next one swung. Below, no sooner was the danger over than another dilemma arose, in that they couldn't detach the falls; the water was so calm there was no lift. The boat drifted aft, still caught, and again the women wailed. The second boat was falling now, directly above the first. A voice called out, 'For God's sake, she'll scuttle us,' and then the helmsman must have used his knife for the next instant the boat swerved and slid free.

I wasn't cold any more, that's for sure; the sweat ran into

my eyes. Hopper had a split lip. We went up top to see what more could be done and found a collapsible had been hitched to the empty davits where the Duff Gordons' boat had hung. Mr Carter and Bruce Ismay stood beside it. They had their hands cupped to their mouths and were bellowing for women to come forward, but there didn't seem to be any in sight. I shouted that there were plenty on the decks below and with that the officer helped Mr Carter and Mr Ismay on board. Mr Carter called out for Hopper and me to join them, but we shook our heads. I can't know for certain what Hopper was thinking, yet I guess we both felt it would be an unmanly thing to do with so many women still stranded. Mr Carter wasn't a bad old stick and I didn't want him to feel we'd shown him up, so I ran to the rail and wished him God Speed and said I hoped to see him and Mrs Carter before long. Such was the list of the ship that as the collapsible dropped it banged against the hull and they had to lever it away with the oars for fear the rivet-heads tore the canvas. We could hear Ismay yelling for Mr Carter to put his back into it.

We were hurrying aft when Hopper spied Charlie sitting on a bench at the base of the second funnel. He was cradling Wallis in his arms. 'She won't stop shaking,' he said. 'Rosenfelder's given her his coat but it hasn't made any difference.' Guiltily, I remembered my promise. I told him not to move from the spot, not unless he could manage to get Wallis into a life-boat. He pursed his mouth and said that was unlikely. He had tried to do just that ten minutes before and she'd bitten his hand.

Scurra was still in the Palm Court. The man with the

bottle of Gordon's gin had joined him; he was middle-aged and had mild, if somewhat inflamed, blue eyes. The bottle was almost empty but Scurra hadn't been drinking.

'Wallis needs you,' I said. 'She has to talk to you.' There didn't seem any point in beating about the bush.

'About anything in particular?'

'Come now,' I cried. 'You know damn well what I mean.'

'Is this a private conversation?' asked the gin drinker.

'What would you like me to say to her?' Scurra said. 'What would you advise?' His expression was grave, which took the steam out of me.

'I don't know,' I said. 'Perhaps you could pretend to –'

'If it is,' our table companion interrupted, 'I can always go away. I'm used to going away. I can tip-toe away like a fairy.'

'Pretend what?' Scurra asked.

'To care,' I said.

'It's dangerous to pretend –'

'But if it gets her into the boats –'

'And what if she should survive?' he said. 'No doubt I would then be faced with a breach of promise case.' Now he shook with laughter, but I reckoned it wasn't genuine.

'Perhaps all she wants is for you to say goodbye.'

'Just say the word,' muttered the drinker, his head sinking to the table.

'There's not much time,' I said. 'She's sitting up there, refusing to enter the boats. Do you want her on your conscience?' He said slowly, 'I'm not entirely sure I have one.' He looked away, trying to find an argument. I couldn't force him to go with me, I knew that. The drunk was dreaming, snorting. Scurra patted his head like a mother.

I was prepared to give up when he said, 'I'm not as cruel as you think, you know. I do have my feelings, though they appear to be different from those generally considered suitable. There are many women on this ship who would have granted me their favours, just as there are many men who stepped into the breach once it became obvious I was not available. I say this without vanity, hard as it is for someone of your age and disposition to believe. I am simply stating a fact. I chose Wallis because I recognised a creature similar to myself, that is, in matters of the heart. I use the phrase loosely, you understand, for in a liaison such as I describe the heart is usually absent.'

'Then you chose wrong,' I said hotly. 'She's fearfully upset.'

'That is because of unfortunate circumstances,' he reasoned. 'I didn't expect to couple with death so soon after engaging in what passes for love.'

'I don't want to hear it,' I shouted, and I meant death, not the other thing, of which I knew nothing.

'Supposing I come with you,' he argued, 'and do as you say. Ten to one she'll rebuff me. Women are like that, don't you agree? And if I say those comforting words, which have no basis in truth, she may spend the rest of her life deceived into believing that the best has gone for ever, simply because this night is like no other.'

I could stand it no longer and jumped to my feet. 'Goodbye,' I said. 'There is nothing more to say.'

'Goodbye,' echoed the drunk, struggling upright. 'Delighted to have met you.'

All the same, Scurra came with me. I led him to Charlie who had remained at his post with Wallis in his arms. He and I stood a little way off to give them privacy. Poor old Charlie was blue with cold, and mystified, but he held his tongue. We could hear a hubbub of angry voices coming from the port side and women screaming.

I don't know what Scurra said to her. At one point she lifted her hand as though to slap his face and he caught her wrist to stop her. After no more than a few minutes she rose and came over to Charlie. She had recovered her poise and even something of her vivacity. She said matter-of-factly, 'I'm ready to go now,' and tugged the collar of Rosenfelder's fur coat more snugly about her ears.

'Ships that pass in the night,' murmured Scurra, as he sauntered back inside. It was then that I heard the second gun-shot, followed by several more, and a scream louder than all the rest.

*

I didn't recognise Rosenfelder right away because Adele knelt over him, holding his head against her breast and shielding his face with her hand. We prised her away from him, fearful he might be trampled underfoot by the mob who raged about the collapsible now being lowered towards the deck. Between us Charlie and I got him to the nearest bench and laid him down. He wasn't badly hurt but he squealed like a stuck pig when I handled his shoul-

213

der too roughly. He said he'd been endeavouring to get Adele closer to the boat when an officer had begun firing wildly into the crowd. Another officer had tried to take the gun off him because of the women, but by then it was too late. He thought he had been hit in the upper part of the arm.

I left Charlie in charge of him and, ordering Adele and Wallis to hold on tight to the tails of my coat, thrust my way into the centre of that frenzied throng. Groans and curses accompanied my every struggling inch. The list was so bad now that people fell over and were stepped upon and we didn't care. In an attempt to stop all but the women from boarding the officers had linked arms in a circle about the boat. Fortunately, one of them recognised me from my labours on the enclosed promenade and gestured me on. When I reached him I swung the girls round, Wallis first, and he pulled her through. I was in the process of thrusting Adele to safety when that damn gun went off again and in the surge backwards lost my place and was swept to the perimeter. Adele trembled like a leaf and appeared quite incapable of going forward again and, indeed, I too felt I didn't have it in me, for I was exhausted. I had to half carry her back to the bench. Her cloak had been torn off and the front of her gown was smeared with blood, though it was Rosenfelder's not hers. She sat shivering beside the wounded tailor; wincing, he eased himself out of his jacket and draped it about her shoulders. 'You go on,' he said to me. 'I expect you have things to do.'

'If I find there's another boat,' I told him, 'I'll come back for you and Adele.' He nodded. I didn't say goodbye to him, not until later, and I was sorry for it, for when I did he couldn't hear me.

*

We walked towards the stern. Midships, another collapsible was edging its way down to the water. It appeared fairly full. As we watched it go a figure climbed on to the rail beneath, stepped out, and sliding rather than leaping landed half over the gunwale. His head was in the water and when they jerked him upright and he fell on his back we saw it was Ginsberg, insensible and still clutching his sticky handkerchief. I guess his fall had knocked the breath out of him. For a moment it crossed my mind that I too might make a jump for it, but already the boat was moving out of the lights. 'Rats always leave a sinking ship,' remarked Charlie, and I thought that damned unfair, and stupidly told him so. His eyes filled up with tears. Hopper went over to the officer who had just come down from the davits and asked him what we should do. 'Pray,' was the reply.

Now that all the boats had gone, the waiting began. We went inside to search for something that we might cling to in the water. This was Hopper's idea. It was ten minutes to two by the clock on the Grand Staircase and we marvelled that time had crept so slowly, for it seemed we had lived a life-time in the space of an hour.

The card players had remained stoically at their table in the smoke-room. Hopper asked one of them for a cigarette and was told there were hundreds in the bar and all free. He came back with the ornamental lifebuoy that had hung on the wall above the spirits shelf. He tried to put it on but it wouldn't go further than his shoulders, which pinned his arms to his sides so that he couldn't get it off again. In spite of everything, this made me laugh out loud, at which the card players had the cheek to tick me off for being rowdy.

Then I remembered Rosenfelder telling me that they sold souvenirs of the voyage in the barber's shop on C deck. He'd bought a shaving brush with the White Star flag enamelled on the handle. I'd asked him, thinking of Sissy's baby, if they had anything suitable for small children, and he'd said he'd seen teddy bears and inflatable rings for sea-side excursions. I suggested to Charlie that he come with me but he turned pale at the idea of going so far below. 'I'm sorry,' he said, 'I can't help being a coward.' I didn't show it, but I lost patience with him. After all, most of us are cowards, but it's simply not on to shout it from the roof-tops.

It was eerie passing down through the ship. There was no one about, and still all the lights blazed. I didn't use the elevator for fear there was a sudden stagger and I got trapped. The tilt was pronounced now and I walked along the corridors with my hands braced on either side of the walls. When I came to the barber's shop the door was swinging inwards on its hinges. Riley sat in one of the swivel chairs, combing his hair in the mirror. He grinned when he saw me, and spun himself round and round. 'Try it,' he said. 'It's a good lark.' I took the chair next to him and we both whirled. Truly, I felt very much at ease.

'What are you after down here?' he said. 'Did you think you needed a shave?'

'I was looking for something to hold on to … when we hit the water.'

'Get away with you,' he scoffed. 'You'll have her whole bloody innards to choose from once she starts to plunge.' My eyes must have held a shadow of alarm, for he added, 'She won't go just yet, take it from me. Maybe half an hour, longer if we're lucky.'

'Had it anything to do with the fire?' I asked. 'The one in the bunker.'

'Doubt it,' he said. 'We was just going too fast and not heeding the ice warnings.'

'Is the *Carpathia* really on its way?'

'So the Marconi fellow has it. But she won't get to us till the morning.'

'It is the morning.'

'Proper morning,' he said. 'Brekky time.' He stopped spinning and began to unscrew the stoppers of the bottles above the basin, sniffing the contents in turn. When the smell didn't meet with his approval he emptied the liquid down the plug hole. An aroma of scented soap hung in the air. Reflected in the mirror a row of teddy bears sat stiff on the shelf behind me. They wore white sailor hats but the band about each crown bore the letters, backwards, RMS *Olympic*.

'I suppose it's best to jump,' I said. 'And from the stern.'

'Wrong, bloody wrong. Best place is the roof of the officers' house. Where the collapsible is. Her bows will go down and the sea will wash you off. Mind you, the first funnel will likely keep you company.'

'There's another boat?'

'The officers is keeping it for themselves. Leastways, we weren't told to get it down.' He was watching me in the mirror, studying my build. 'You might make it,' he said. 'You'd think the fat ones would do best, having more flesh on them, but mostly their tickers give up under the shock. Now me, I'm on the scrawny side, but that only means the cold will freeze my blood quicker.' I reckoned he was trying to frighten me and stared him out. I asked, 'What did I do to make you so angry ... before?'

'It's water under the bridge now,' he said.

'All the same, I'd like to know.'

'That bleeding half-crown you tossed me.' I stared at him. I thought he meant that in tipping him I'd treated him as an inferior. 'I'm sorry,' I stammered. 'I didn't think.'

'No, you bloody well didn't. Still, it don't matter now ... you with your millions and me with me half-crown, we're both in the same boat.' And with that he took a silver coin out of his pocket and dropped it in the sink. Then he went out of the door. I sat there a moment, feeling sick. I think it was the smell of lavender, not his treatment of me that turned my stomach. I left the coin where it lay, in case he came back, but when I went out into the passage there was no sign of him.

All the way up to A deck I argued with him in my head, protesting that I wasn't stingy and that on his wages I wouldn't have turned my nose up at two shillings and sixpence – but then, I thought of the money Charlie had said I'd thrown away at cards the night before and fairly burned with shame.

Hopper and Charlie had gone from the smoke-room. So

had the card players. Thomas Andrews was standing with his back to me at the fire, balancing up on his toes, positioning a picture in place above the mantelpiece. It was the Plymouth Harbour painting, the one I'd last seen hanging in the library. He stepped back to see if it hung straight, and I called out his name. He didn't turn round. His life-preserver lay across the table. I went closer and said, 'Will you not come up on deck, sir? There isn't much time.' Still with his back to me he fluttered his hand in the air, either waving me away or waving goodbye.

I did as Riley had told me and once on the boat deck climbed the companionway up to the officers' house which was forward of the first funnel. There were seamen on the roof, struggling to release the collapsible. I peered down and saw Guggenheim and his valet both dressed as though off to a swell party. They were listening to the orchestra which was playing rag-time to raise our spirits, Guggenheim tap-tapping his cane on the rail. Hopper stood not a yard from them, looking first one way then the other. I guessed he was trying to find me and shouted to him. By good luck he heard and sprinted towards the stairs. He told me Charlie was further along the deck. They had both gone aft to where a priest was giving conditional absolution to a demented congregation. When Charlie had fallen to his knees and started to blub out the most damn fool confessions, like how he'd tormented a cat when he was a child and how he'd stolen a dollar from his mother's purse, he had to leave him. 'Honest to God, Morgan, he's turned yellow.'

At that moment the orchestra changed tune and struck

up a hymn, one I knew well because it was a favourite of my aunt's and sometimes she used to sing it when she was in one of her brighter moods ... *E'en though it be a cross that raiseth me, Still all my song shall be, Nearer my God to Thee, Nearer to Thee.* Hearing it, I knew I had to go in search of Charlie, for Lady Melchett's sake if not my own, and would have gone on searching for him if Scurra hadn't been waiting for me at the bottom of the steps. He said, 'A man bears the weight of his own body without knowing it, but he soon feels the weight of any other object. There is nothing, absolutely nothing, that a man cannot forget – but not himself.' Then, before walking away, he said those other things, about it being the drop, not the height, that was terrible, and I left Charlie to God and went back up to the officers' house.

And now, the moment was almost upon us. The stern began to lift from the water. Guggenheim and his valet played mountaineers, going hand over hand up the rail. The hymn turned ragged; ceased altogether. The musicians scrambled upwards, the spike of the cello scraping the deck. Clinging to the rung of the ladder I tried to climb to the roof but there was such a sideways slant that I waved like a flag on a pole. I thought I must make a leap for it and turned to look for Hopper. Something, some inner voice urged me to glance below and I saw Scurra again, one arm hooked through the rail to steady himself. I raised my hand in greeting – then the water, first slithering, then tumbling, gushed us apart.

As the ship staggered and tipped, a great volume of water flowed in over the submerged bows and tossed me like a cork to the roof. Hopper was there too. My fingers touched some kind of bolt near the ventilation grille and I grabbed it tight. I filled my lungs with air and fixed my eyes on the blurred horizon, determined to hang on until I was sure I could float free rather than be swilled back and forth in a maelstrom. I wouldn't waste my strength in swimming, not yet, for I knew the ship was now my enemy and if I wasn't vigilant would drag me with her to the grave. I waited for the next slithering dip and when it came and the waves rushed in and swept me higher, I released my grip and let myself be carried away, over the tangle of ropes and wires and davits, clear of the rails and out into the darkness. I heard the angry roaring of the dying ship, the deafening cacophony as she stood on end and all her guts tore loose. I choked on soot and cringed beneath the sparks dancing like fire-flies as the forward funnel broke and smashed the sea in two. I thought I saw Hopper's face but one eye was ripped away and he gobbled like a fish on the hook. I was sucked under, as I knew I would be, down, down, and still I waited, waited until the pull slackened – then I struck out with all my strength.

I don't know how long I swam under that lidded sea – time had stopped with my breath – and just as it seemed as if my lungs would burst the blackness paled and I kicked to the surface. I had thought I was entering paradise, for I was alive and about to breathe again, and then I heard the cries of souls in torment and believed myself in hell. Dear God! Those voices! *Father ... Father ... For the love of Christ ... Help me, for pity's sake! ... Where is my son*. Some called for their mothers, some on the Lord, some to die quickly, a few to be saved. The lamentations rang through the frosty air and touched the stars; my own mouth opened in a silent howl of grief. The cries went on and on, trembling, lingering – and God forgive me, but I wanted them to end. In all that ghastly night it was the din of the dying that chilled the most. Presently, the voices grew fainter, ceased – yet still I heard them, as though the drowned called to one another in a ghostly place where none could follow. Then silence fell, and that was the worst sound of all. There was no trace of the *Titanic*. All that remained was a grey veil of vapour drifting above the water.

Gradually I grew accustomed to the darkness and made out a boat some distance away. Summoning up all my strength I swam closer; it was a collapsible, wrong side up and sagging in the sea. I tried to climb on to the gunwale but the occupants gazed through me and offered no assistance; they might have been dead men for all the life in their eyes. Swimming round to the far side, I commandeered a bobbing barrel, and, mounting it like a horse, hand-paddled to the stern and flung myself aboard.

We slushed there, twenty or more of us, lying like sponges in the icy pond within that canvas bag, looking up at the stars, students of the universe, each man lost in separate thoughts and dreams. I saw the library and that figure now clinging to the tilted mantelpiece, and old man Seefax, arms raised in terror as his chair skidded the room and the water leapt to douse the coals. Then I was in London again standing outside the Café Royal, the wet pavement shining in the lamp-light, a bunch of violets in my hand. And as I waited the revolving doors began to spin and out they came – Hopper, smiling, asking where the devil I'd been;

Ginsberg, slapping me on the back in greeting; Charlie, cheeks pink with pleasure at the sight of me; Ben Guggenheim with his top hat jaunty on his head; Riley, hands in pockets, jingling coins; lastly, Scurra, staying within the doors, now facing me, now showing me his back, then facing me again, eyes sadly fixed on mine. Each time he passed he made an upward gesture with his hand and I stepped to join him, but the doors spun round and round and when they slowed he'd gone. Then Charlie pointed to the sky and we all looked up to watch a shooting star.

Now it was very cold in the boat and we were sinking deeper as we floated. I sat up and rubbed my frozen limbs, shouting at the others to stir themselves unless they wished to die. Some grumbled and resisted but most saw the sense in it and we worked together, baling out as much water as we could, though we still sat in that icy pool and sloped alarmingly. Fearing we might be swamped I organised them to stand up, not all at once, but in twos and separated by the length of an arm to maintain a balance. When this was accomplished and we all faced the horizon someone declared there was a ship out there and that she was moving. We stared as hard as we could, but there was such a display of shooting stars that night it was difficult to distinguish one light from another. An hour crept by, and to our delight we heard voices. Pretty soon, by means of shouting back and forth, two life-boats loomed. There was space in one of them for three of us, but we daren't disturb our balance and they rowed off.

It must have been thirty minutes or so later when that second lot of shooting stars went arching to the sea. We gazed in disbelief because they burst asunder before they fell. A solitary cheer came from somewhere to our right and a woman's voice shouted, 'It's the *Carpathia* for sure.' For one instant I wanted to cheer too, the next that momentary leap of relief was replaced by unease which deepened into guilt, for in that moment I had already begun to forget the dead. Now that I knew I was going to live there was something dishonourable in survival.

Dawn came and as far as the eye could see the ocean was dotted with islands and fields of ice. Some floated with tapering mast-heads, some sailed with monstrous bows rising sheer to the pink-flushed sky, some glided the water in the shapes of ancient vessels. Between this pale fleet the little life-boats rocked. There were other things caught upon the water – chairs and tables, crates, an empty gin bottle, a set of bagpipes, a cup without a handle, a creased square of canvas with a girl's face painted on it; and two bodies, she in a gown of ice with a mermaid's tail, he in shirt sleeves, the curls stiff as wood shavings on his head, his two hands frozen to the curve of a metal rail. Beyond, where the sun was beginning to show its burning rim, smoke blew from a funnel.